Praise for Shimmer & Other Stories

"The best writers, like the best wines, just get better. Lori L. Lake has always been a master craftsperson, but she gets better every time she steps up to the plate. Her most recent novel, Snow Moon Rising, garnered a long list of well-deserved awards. Now we have this splendid collection of short stories, bold and beautiful, love stories in the broadest, most universal sense and, like those fine wines, to be savored in their complexity, not just short term but over the years as well. These are stories you'll want to read and read again.

Take Me Out is the heartrending story of an unlikely friendship that blooms between a young woman and a very old one. *Tsuki Tsuki* takes a frank look at sexual harassment in some of its more subtle forms. *Paige* tells of one angry, shunned young woman's return from prison, and the redemption she finds in love. *Another Stage* uses a musical production to showcase the anguish of a woman who's not only lost a breast to cancer, but an unsympathetic partner as well. Then there's the title story, *Shimmer*, which does indeed glow with a rapturous light: a generation of gays and lesbians shed their cloaks of invisibility in the wake of the Stonewall uprising.

I'm glad I get the privilege of being the first to predict another round of honors for Miss Lori Lake."

~Victor Banis, author of *Longhorns, Come This Way*, and 140 other novels

"Lake has created distinctive and memorable characters in settings that will linger with readers long after the stories come to their satisfying and hopeful conclusions. Here are five compelling tales of outsiders: women ex-offenders, lesbians, cancer survivors alone with their altered bodies. All bump up against the harsh real world and find salvation in surprising ways, from the supernatural to a former nemesis turned guardian angel."

~Lee Lynch, author of *Sweet Creek, Rafferty Street*, and many other novels

"Lori Lake's 'Take Me Out' is (an)other surprise, in its emotional depth and sensitive exploration of assisted suicide portrayed between a retired schoolteacher and her former student who's now a housekeeper at the senior center where the elderly teacher is slowly dying."
~Twin Cities Daily Planet

"In *Shimmer and Other Stories*, Lori L. Lake serves up a tempting array of treats as her outstanding characters experience the sweetness of true soulmates in Another Stage; handle the sourness of a reproachful town in Paige; admire the tartness of an old lady's gumption in Take Me Out; savor the tastiness of unsuspected friends in Tsuki, Tsuki; and overthrow the bitterness of discrimination in Shimmer. Sample these delightful morsels. Lake has laid out a feast."
~Nann Dunne, Editor-in-Chief of JustAboutWrite.com

About Lori's Previous Collection
Stepping Out

"Some writers write stories and have fun. In this collection, Lake fell in love with her characters. She cared for and nurtured them, making this not so much a collection of stories as an anthology of characters."
~Lambda Book Report

"Each of the short stories is timeless and authentic in its portrayal of real people and their lives . . . Each story brings forth a wisdom that we all should possess as we go through life."
~The Independent Gay Writer

"Each of the fourteen stories is emotive and evocative, and ultimately satisfying, leaving readers charmed and wishing some of these were longer."
~Blissengine Review

Shimmer

and

Other Stories

Lori L. Lake

Portland, Oregon

Portland, Oregon
www.LaunchPointPress.com

Table of Contents

Acknowledgments, 2022

Though this book has always been obtainable in ebook form, it hasn't been available in print for a number of years. I am so happy to get it back out for people to read.

In the time since this book was first published, I've lost Betty Crandall, a wonderful friend through thick and thin; the world has lost the iconoclastic and exceptional voice of Victor Banis; and the insightful Nann Dunne has had to retire from editing due to serious health issues. I miss all of them immensely and intensely.

At times, I also miss my former partner of 27 years. Diane and I parted in late 2008, and I moved back to my old hometown in Oregon while she stayed in Minnesota. I continue to be thankful to Diane for all the support she gave regarding my writing career. If it weren't for her, I'm not sure that I'd have believed in myself enough to make the Writing Road my career. It's one thing to have a passion for something and quite another to make a living at it. Diane was one of many who believed in me, and I'll always be appreciative of that.

When people are taken away, for whatever reason, I've always found that new ones eventually slide into their place, and I'm happy to say Claudia Kuzie has been a terrific new friend. So glad to have her as a comrade and neighbor here at the Fortress of Solitude.

Last but never least—saving the best for last, I should say—I feel such happiness and gratitude for my very special Fairy Godmother, Lee Lynch. Over the last fifteen years she's been my wise Tribal Elder dispensing advice, wisdom and hope on a regular basis. She has made my life better and the Writing Road less lonely. Long may she run! (Or walk swiftly, anyway. ☺)

Lori L. Lake
Portland, Oregon
June 2022

Acknowledgments, 2007

Thanks to the online venues and editors that provide an outlet for short fiction, especially Claudia Wilde and Carrie Tierney at Khimairal Ink magazine and Aldo Alvarez and Eric Anderson at Blithe House Quarterly. Much appreciation to Norton Stillman of Nodin Press and Ellen Hart, William Kent Krueger, and Carl Brookins of the Minnesota Crime Wave who graciously accepted "Take Me Out" for the *Silence of the Loons* anthology. Thanks to Kathy L. Smith for the opportunity to edit the *Romance For Life* anthology.

Kudos to the following people for writing advice, editing, and encouragement during the creation of these stories: Ann Bannon, Betty Crandall, Brenda Adcock, Catherine Friend, Elaine Mulligan, Ellen Hart, Jane Vollbrecht, Jim Friel, Joyce McNeil, Laura Lively, Lee Lynch, Nann Dunne, Patty Schramm, Verda Foster, and last but not least, Victor Banis. Proofreading honors go to Patty Schramm, Mary Phillips, and Bette McLaughlin.

Above all else, I thank Diane, who makes my life shimmer with possibilities, and who has stood beside me every step of the way down this Writing Road, even though I'm not always so good with the map.

Lori L. Lake
Autumn, 2007
Twin Cities, Minnesota

Foreword by Ann Bannon

This collection of five stories by Lori L. Lake is about familiar people living familiar lives, with one important difference: in Lake's hands, they are anything but ordinary and sometimes downright magical. She is a keen observer of the telling detail, be it a bit of clothing, a perfectly named character, a sound, or the expression on a human face, and she can find the words to inspirit them with life. She's a superb seat-of-the-pants linguist and she puts all of her skills to work in the service of her engaging stories.

These tales are bubbling with the energy of real people wrestling with their devils, facing up to their own errors, and discovering their true worth. In one ("Another Stage"), a lopsided love affair is dying. A young woman who thinks that her heart, like her body, will never be patched, reluctantly helps out a friend and gets an astonishing reward. In "Paige," a girl just released from prison tries to come back to her hometown and is nearly suffocated by the scorn of unforgiving townsfolk. But love can bloom anywhere, even in a candy shop, a school gym, or the heart of an ex-con. "Take Me Out, gives us an old lady full of wonderful stories and a child's love of learning, who takes a lost soul to her heart and makes the young woman see the unexpected wonders already within her grasp.

"Shimmer," the title story, takes us back to a dark past to look at life through the eyes of those who were young in the months leading up to the 1969 Stonewall Rebellion. It seems so far away now as to be almost unreal. But under the wing of Lake's surprising heroine, a girl who learns how to work the "shimmer," we get a guided tour of the events of the era. And we learn a new respect for those who found their courage back then. The story is aptly dedicated to the wonderful Victor Banis, pioneer extraordinaire in the field of gay male pulp fiction.

In these artfully written stories, many of the characters who thought they had given up on happiness find it coming at them from the least likely corners of their world. Lake has a flawless ear for the witty twists of the English language and a fine grasp of popular culture. She fearlessly situates her characters in a range of places, times, and dilemmas that might daunt a less gifted and confident author. Readers can relax, knowing they will be carried along by a born storyteller.

Mark Twain says that if you need to include an old lady screaming in your story, don't tell us about her—drag her on-stage and let her scream. Lori L. Lake has learned that lesson brilliantly, as her bouquet of prestigious awards attests. Among them is the very first Ann Bannon Popular Choice Award, given to her in June of 2007. It confirms my suspicion that Lake's readers recognize pure gold when they find it.

Ann Bannon
Sacramento, California
November, 2007

Dedicated to all the pioneering gay and lesbian authors who have led the way for me and for so many others, and, in particular, to these twelve trailblazers whose work is near and dear to my heart:

Ann Bannon
Ann Allen Shockley
Ellen Hart
Jane Rule
Joseph Hansen
Katherine V. Forrest
Lee Lynch
Marijane Meaker/ME Kerr/Vin Packer
Patricia Nell Warren
Rita Mae Brown
Sandra Scoppettone
Victor Banis

"Some women wait for something
to change and nothing
does change
so they change
themselves."

Audre Lord, "Stations,"
Our Dead Behind Us (1986)

TAKE ME OUT

When is a crime also a sin, and when is that sin unforgivable? If you commit a crime and don't get caught, and only God knows what you've done, does that lessen the penalty phase at the Gates of St. Peter?

Kaye Brock had puzzled over such issues for most of her adulthood, and as she drove through icy streets to her housekeeping job, she wondered most about this: if you aren't sorry about what you've done, does it stay on your heavenly record, like the black cigarette residue left on a smoker's lungs? Surely this was a question for the priests, but it had been eight years, right after her senior year in high school, since she'd been to St. Bertold's Catholic Church, and she had no intention of returning to discuss her concerns. Still, she wondered.

On this gloomy, sub-zero morning, Kaye hustled out of her old Ford Taurus, pulling her coat tight around her. The skies threatened snow. Already the wind was bitter. As she walked toward the entrance to Seaton Senior Center, everything was etched in bright and bitter outlines. Dead plant stalks stood in stark relief against the stucco to the right of the handicap entrance. It was a barren, hopeless time for Kaye and had felt so for far too long. She sighed, and her moist breath created a swirling fog around her face.

Her glasses misted up upon entering the building. The eighty-degree temperature difference between the outdoors and the huge meeting area through which she strolled caused her to break out in a light sweat as it had every morning since winter had descended.

Kaye passed the main office, careful to look away from the ever-present face behind the desk in the glassed-in area. The assistant administrator, Sheila Thornton, knew all about Kaye's sordid history and had never shared so much as one smile with her. It didn't seem fair to Kaye, especially since her crime had been a victimless one, and she had fully paid her debt to society. She'd served nearly four years of her seven-year sentence, and her parole would soon be over. She'd returned home to find that the idea of debts being settled didn't matter to a surprisingly large number of people in town. Old school acquaintances looked away in the Target store. The servers in the café ignored her. Nobody spoke to her but gossip hounds and those new to Melville.

She reached Advanced Care and thumbed the door release. This was placed high enough that the residents, most of whom were in wheelchairs, couldn't reach it and make their escape into the world of the living.

Inside the hot and humid unit, the odors of a eucalyptus plant and industrial-strength, pine-scented floor cleaner battled to cover up the underlying reek of urine and feces. When she'd first joined the AC staff, the smell had nearly overpowered her. She'd worked through those first shifts on the edge of nausea. But after a few weeks, she grew accustomed to the odor, and now it was merely an ever-present reminder of decay and sadness and loss. Not much different from prison.

Kaye shed her gloves, coat, and muffler, carrying them over her arm as she headed down the long hallway on the right. She was early and could afford to take her time, perhaps slip out back and sneak a smoke before her shift began.

"Hi, Kaye," one of the aides, Susie, said from behind the charge nurse's counter.

Kaye smiled at her, but before she could say anything, the ambulance bay opened and let in a gust of refreshing chilled air.

"Easy does it," a man said in a loud voice.

Kaye stopped at the charge nurse's tall counter and watched the attendants pull a gurney out of the wagon. One medic rolled it into the hallway while the other closed up the ambulance and quickly shut the extra-wide hospital door.

Nurse Judy and a hulking aide named Marcus moved down the hall and stopped on either side of the gurney. "Well, hello," the nurse said, in a baby voice. "Let's get you all warmed up and settled, sweetie pie."

The attendant came forward, holding out a clipboard to Judy. "Here's Gildecott for you. Sign off?"

"That's *Missus* Gildecott to you, young man." It took a moment for Kaye to realize the imperious voice emanated from the stretcher. "Don't think I don't remember your abysmal manners from sophomore English."

The man flushed bright red. He squinted and leaned down to look at the figure swathed in blankets. "Mrs.—Mrs.—"

"That's right, James McVie. I never forget a face. Never."

Wide-eyed, the medic reached across the gurney and took back his clipboard. "You folks have a great day."

He and the other medic rushed away so quickly that Kaye tensed. She looked down the hall, hoping they wouldn't run over any of the wheelchair occupants.

Judy said, "Well, then, Mrs. Gildecott, Susie and Marcus and I will get you settled."

"A most excellent idea. And I don't care for baby talk. This is not childcare. I do hope they have brought me to an adult care facility."

"Oh, yes, ma'am," Judy said.

Kaye stepped out of the way. Marcus released the lock on the gurney and gave it a gentle push. As the entourage rolled by, a pair of dark, bright eyes, glittering with anger, looked up at Kaye, holding her gaze as she passed. Mrs. Gildecott. Kaye's high school English teacher and the terror of Melville Secondary School. Kaye swallowed with difficulty. Suddenly she needed nicotine—badly. She clutched her coat tight against her and headed toward the back door, keyed the code, and stepped outdoors. Mrs. Gildecott was coming to live here? What a nightmare.

Kaye stood stamping and sucking nervously on a Winston outside the back door of the AC Unit. Mrs. Gildecott. Jesus. She remembered sitting in Mythology class, terrified she would be called on. She liked to read about individual gods like Artemis, Apollo, Minerva, and Poseidon, but she couldn't keep track of who was related to who or whether they were Greek or Roman. Mostly she remembered keeping a low profile. She recalled a time when Mrs. Gildecott waited in the hall before class one day, and Larry Knoche held court at the front desk near the door. Pointing at their textbook, he'd made off-color comments about Dido, queen of Carthage, calling her "Dildo" and laughing uproariously with his buddies. Next thing Kaye knew, tiny Mrs. Gildecott was behind Larry. The nearly six-foot kid shot up from his desk as though his chair had exploded. He was dragged to the door by one ear, thrown into the hall like day-old rubbish, and never seen again in Mythology class.

Kaye remembered the thrill of terror and satisfaction she had felt. Larry Knoche was a popular kid with a mean streak. She hadn't been sorry to see him go and no one else complained, not even his buddies. In the four years she was at Melville High, Kaye learned nobody crossed Mrs. G. If you didn't behave in her class, she threw you out. Simple as that.

And now she was at Seaton Center.

The center was far more than an old folks' home. The administrators spoke of it as a "campus," as though the place were an expensive institution for antique teenagers. At one end was the elevator entrance to a twelve-story high-rise. Ninety apartments thrust up from the Minnesota prairie to serve as "Independent Living" for couples and singles aged sixty and older. When the day came that occupants could no longer fend for themselves, they came down from their ivory tower and moved into a connected four-story facility. "Assisted Living" sported smaller rooms, but meals were provided as well as cleaning, laundry, medication dispensing, and round-the-clock monitoring.

When Kaye first applied to work at Seaton three years earlier, Sheila Thornton had made it clear she would not be trusted in either of those facilities where people still kept sums of money, jewelry, and valuables. Never mind that Kaye no longer had any interest in theft. No statute of limitations existed with the Sheila Thorntons of the world, so Kaye was assigned to Advanced Care. No fancy "Living" name was attached to Seaton's AC section. Apparently, you literally came down in the world from the high-rise to the low-rise and then at last to the ground floor which was, quite simply, a nursing home. If euphemisms hadn't been so important to the families of the patients in the AC Unit, Kaye thought it would be more aptly named "Assisted Dying."

She pulled her unzipped coat tight, one arm crossed over her chest, and took a deep drag. During inclement weather, nobody used this back area. When the weather was nice, residents and staff were all over the gardened enclosure, which had no exit and prevented confused patients from wandering away. But the roses were long gone now, and the path leading to an eight-foot-tall wrought iron fence was iced over. Bushes and shrubbery in the flowerbeds were also shrouded with ice. In spring and summer, Kaye often came out to sit on the tiny white bench tucked in an alcove to the right of the door. Surrounded by roses, iris, and tiger lilies, she liked to watch the bees buzzing from flower to flower as the warmth of the sun bathed her face. Not today. She shivered as she took a final pull on the cigarette.

The glass door behind her jerked open, and a murder of crows, lined up along the gutter overhead, startled and flew upward, cawing raucously.

"Brock!" Marcus's light brown face squinted out into the breeze. "Another big shit attack from your favorite, Mister Clancy." The door slammed shut, and the last intrepid crow took flight. A murder of crows, a gaggle of geese, a pride of lions—Kaye wondered what a bunch of elderly, wheelchair-bound people would be called. An exaltation of elderly? No, that was larks. Maybe a dejection—or desolation—of elders.

Kaye dropped the cigarette on the sidewalk, not even bothering to grind it out, and followed Marcus's football physique into the hothouse. She stopped at the housekeeping closet and prepared the mop and rolling bucket. Mister Clancy had a serious bowel problem, and nearly every day she started out her shift cleaning up one of his "accidents." She rolled the bucket down the hallway, weaving her way around frail old ladies sitting in wheelchairs outside their rooms. She was constantly amazed at how Mrs. Adler and Mrs. Johanssen could sleep, their heads canted off at angles that made them look like someone had come along behind them and broken their necks. And Mrs. Polnicek always managed to fold forward like origami, her gray head resting on her knees and the knuckles of her skinny hands brushing the metal footrests of her chair. Just looking at her made Kaye's back hurt.

The morning passed slowly in a zen-like trance of mopping left, mopping right, wiping down surfaces, sweeping, vacuuming. Kaye slipped into a fog of numbness, humming old

R.E.M. and Nirvana songs. The AC Unit consisted of two long hallways connected at either end by short hallways. They formed one big circle, and a few of the wheelchair occupants spent their days rolling 'round and 'round it. The lunchroom, various offices, rehab, storage centers, and nursing stations were situated down the middle with the patient suites along the outside walls. Each room contained two or three residents. Kaye worked her way through the eighteen suites on the left side of the unit, then took her lunch break. Afterwards, she started in on the sunroom and the eighteen rooms on the right. She hadn't gotten far when she came to the room occupied by Mrs. Gildecott.

The old woman lay at a slight incline on the small hospital bed. When Kaye had last seen her at Melville High, Mrs. Gildecott sported a cap of swirling silver hair, all of which was now white as snow. Her hands gripped the top of the coverlet, and her mouth was open slightly. Kaye started her cleaning in the open bathroom area just inside the door. The other three corners of the room contained small bays for beds. The left rear bay was currently unoccupied, and Mrs. Gildecott lay in the front right bay separated from Mrs. Hoffmeier by a thin curtain. The two women's beds were head-to-head, close to the curtain. Kaye didn't understand why the nurses set them up like that. Three-quarters of the elderly people in the home snored like beached walruses. She thought it made more sense to put the heads of the beds as far away from one another as possible. But who was she to say? It wasn't like her opinion was respected.

Kaye didn't like to get to know any of the residents, other than by name. Too many of them died quickly, and the ones who lingered on grew sicker as each day passed. The lucky few who were only temporarily placed for rehab came and went as their broken hips or pneumonias healed. The rest served life sentences of pain and confusion that Kaye tried not to think about.

She sprayed harsh industrial-strength window cleaner on the mirror and expertly wiped it down. On the last sweep with the cloth, she caught sight of a movement behind her and met dark eyes, staring across the room.

Mrs. Gildecott cleared her throat. "Kaye Lynn Brock."

Kaye couldn't speak. Her heart thumped, and she reached back to steady herself on the sink's cold porcelain.

Mrs. Gildecott gazed out the window. "The snow is lovely. I surely wish you could take me out. I always loved sledding and a bonfire on a snowy night."

"Last I checked, ma'am, the temp was hovering at zero.
You'll have to wait until spring."

"Yes, spring." She fastened her dark eyes on Kaye once more, seeming to look right through her. "You had an imaginative flair, but you couldn't spell to save your life."

Kaye swallowed. "Nope, and I still can't."

Mrs. Gildecott dug her elbows in on either side of her and inched herself up to a more erect position. She reached up a hand to smooth her hair. "I'm happy to report that many studies were done in the late Nineties, and lack of spelling ability appears to be something with which you are born. No one considers it a moral failing any longer. Have you done anything in the interim—utilized any strategies, I mean—to overcome the problem?"

"Uhh, not really. I have a dictionary." But I never use it, Kaye thought. In fact, I don't bother to write much of anything at all.

"Such a shame, dear. The stories you wrote were inspired. I expected you to go on and write for a newspaper or magazine." Kaye felt a rush of heat flood her face. Working in the writing field had never occurred to her. "I—I've had a different . . . well, that's not the direction I went."

Mrs. Gildecott nodded. "It's never too late to change course. Did you take any college classes after you left Melville High?"

Kaye took a deep breath. She never knew how forthcoming to be about her conviction, and obviously nearly eight years earlier Mrs. Gildecott hadn't followed the front-page news of her arrest. "I worked for a short while in a bank when I got out of school, and I've taken a few correspondence courses." She cleared her throat, purposely omitting the fact that the mail-order courses were all focused in the area of addiction and recovery, and they'd been underwritten by the Shakopee Women's Prison. "I've never gone back to further my education."

"Such a shame, a shame." The old woman closed her eyes and dozed off, leaving Kaye standing against the sink feeling not much better than she had when she'd come before the parole board three years earlier.

The cold weather continued, and Thanksgiving neared. As Kaye mopped the back hall near the laundry room, she tried to mentally prepare herself for the yearly holidays, hoping maybe this would be the year her family—her father and the families of her four older brothers and younger sister—would forgive her for her sins. Her mother had died of a heart attack just after Kaye went to prison, and without exception, the whole clan still blamed Kaye.

"Oh, shit," Marcus mumbled as he rushed out of Mrs. Swanson's room and nearly ran into Kaye.

"Whoa!" She reached out to steady herself against the wall. "What's the matter?"

"Oh, good, Brock, it's you." He lowered his voice. "That old bag and her perfume! She just dropped and busted the whole friggin' bottle. It stinks to the rafters. Stinks so bad my eyes are watering."

"I'll take care of it."

"Thanks." He hustled off one way and she went the other, toward the housekeeping closet. She took a new bag of Tidy Cats kitty litter off the shelf and carried it back to Mrs. Swanson's room. No sooner had she stepped inside the room than the fragrance wafted up, overpowering and cloying. Mrs. Swanson sat in her wheelchair, tears running down her face. The egg-shaped bottle lay on the floor, amber liquid exploded out from it on all sides. The brown lid had bounced across the floor and come to rest under the windows.

"My only bottle. My last bottle. No more, no more," Mrs. Swanson whispered. Her wig was askew. She clenched her fists and pounded on the smooth plastic arms of her chair.

Kaye ripped open the corner of the kitty litter and went down on one knee to pour a generous amount on the perfume. Her eyes smarted, but she knew once the noxious liquid was covered, the intense smell would gradually abate.

"You ruined it," Mrs. Swanson shrieked. "Ruined, ruined, ruined. Not pretty anymore."

Somebody skidded into the doorway. "Brock, whatchu doing?"

Kaye turned to see Sheila Thornton standing behind her. Before she could answer, Nurse Judy came into the room, clucking her tongue. She leaned down and said soothing things in Mrs. Swanson's ear. The old woman's cries subsided, and Nurse Judy went on in a louder voice, "You come with me, sweetie pie. Come on now, and we'll let your room air out." She grabbed for the handles and maneuvered the wheelchair out of the room leaving Kaye and the administrator.

Kaye rose, rolled down the top of the kitty litter bag, and stepped around the other woman.

"Where do you think you're going? I asked you a question." Kaye stopped and glanced into Sheila's baby-blue eyes. Her blonde hair was beautifully coiffed into a high ponytail that was wrapped into a bun on top. Everything about her was elegant and classy, from her bone-thin physique to her smart high heels, designer jacket, skirt, and silk blouse. Kaye looked down at her own light blue uniform top and slacks. A perfume stain splotched the knee of her pants, and sometime during the day, she'd gotten a smear of something disgustingly tan on the sleeve of her smock.

"I had nothing to do with this accident," Kaye said and slipped past.

"If I find out differently, you'll be hearing from me."

Sheila's words followed Kaye down the hall as she lugged the litter bag back to the closet. When she returned to Mrs. Swanson's room with a broom and dustpan, Sheila was gone.

Later that night, in the comfort of her studio apartment, Kaye sat wondering why Sheila Thornton had it in for her. It wasn't like she'd ever touched the woman's purse or bank accounts, and she'd never been anything but polite to her. Kaye had walked into the housekeeping job with strikes against her, and she had no clue how they could be removed.

Kay pushed a dust mop down the hallway. At seven a.m. few residents were stirring, but Mrs. Crocker, bent over with a dowager's hump, slipped around the doorframe of her room like a wraith. "Help," she whispered. "Help me, someone. Help." One narrow, slippered foot slid forward a few inches, then the other, and she made her way by leaning a shoulder against the wall.

Moving the dust mop out of her way, Kaye strode quickly past the hollow-eyed woman.

"I need help," Mrs. Crocker said in a louder voice. "They've stolen everything."

Kaye left her for the aides and nurses. Mrs. Crocker regularly wandered the halls begging for help. She never stopped her pleas all day. When she tired, she headed for the nearest bed—regardless of whether it was occupied—and fell down into a dead sleep. If the elderly woman wasn't circling the premises, saying "Help" like a deranged peacock, she was in someone else's bed.

Kaye wished she'd sleep a great deal more.

A wheelchair emerged from a room up ahead. Mrs. Hoffmeier, haggard and shriveled, sat in the chair, her eyes dull and sleepy as Nurse Judy pushed her. "Brock, I've cleaned up Mrs. Gildecott, but the floor needs mopping. I'm taking Mrs. Hoffmeier down to the sunroom."

"I'll get right on it, Nurse. It'll be cleaned up before she gets back."

Kaye rolled the mop and bucket into room 18. Mrs. Gildecott lay on her side, facing the wall. A pile of linens lay next to her bed. Kaye picked them up and took them out to the laundry barrel. When she returned to the room, Mrs. Gildecott was struggling to roll onto her back.

"Aren't you going to help me?"

"I'm a housekeeper, Mrs. G. I'm not allowed to help you." She grabbed the mop and put the head through the bucket's wringer. "You can alert someone with the call button."

"Never mind. It's not like anyone comes when the button is depressed—even repeatedly. You wouldn't be cleaning up that mess if they had come."

Kaye flicked the mop to the left, then to the right, in the practiced rhythm she had learned well in prison. Mrs. Gildecott struggled, eventually managing to get settled face up.

"Don't you want to know what's wrong with me?"

"I don't ask questions. I'm just the housekeeper."

"Oh, my. Now that's no attitude to have, dear. Surely you're more than that. You have a family? A husband?" Kaye shook her head. "Aspirations? Are you using this job as a steppingstone to other things?"

Kaye smiled and let out a snort. "You find that amusing?"

"Not really." She dunked the mop head back in the bucket and then wrung it out again.

"You are a singularly incurious woman."

Kaye stopped and met the dark eyes surveying her. "All right, then. What are you in for?"

Mrs. Gildecott laughed. "You sound like a gangster, dear." She pitched her voice low and growled out, "What are you in for? You wanna float with the fishes? Make my day." When Kaye laughed, Mrs. Gildecott shook her head. "Just because I'm old doesn't mean I don't pay attention to what's happening around me. And you?"

Kaye smiled. "I don't ask questions. It's not my place. Somebody else is responsible for rounding up the usual suspects. The management has made it very clear that housekeepers are not to bother the residents." Dark eyes studied Kaye, and for a moment she felt vulnerable, as though Mrs. Gildecott could see right through her.

"In that case, Kaye, I shall tell you. I've got the worst case of osteoporosis the doctors have ever seen. I fell and fractured my pelvis last winter. When I saw the X-rays, I was shocked at the images. My bones have turned to chalk, and there's no way to repair them or for me to recover the mobility I've lost. My cousin's son put me up for several months, but now he has developed renal disease and cannot meet my needs. So here I am. End of the line."

Gripping the mop handle with both hands, Kaye leaned forward. "I see. It's a horrible place to stay, you know."

"Actually, this is one of the finest facilities in the state. The rehabilitation department is top-notch, and the rating for patient care and administration is stellar." She paused. "But you're right. It's not so much the facility as it is the circumstances. No intelligent adult should ever be locked up—incontinent, alone, and lonely—in a place like this."

Kaye agreed. Seaton was not a place she ever wanted to be placed. She'd rather go over a cliff first. The image of Geena Davis and Susan Sarandon at the end of Thelma and Louise came to her, and she bit back a smile.

"I had seven good years of retirement, and then it went kaput."

Kaye frowned. "Seven?"

"I can hardly count last year, so yes, a mere seven."

"How old were you when you retired?" Kaye stopped abruptly and blushed. "I'm sorry. That was rude."

"Not at all. Your bluntness is refreshing after the distressing level of baby talk to which I'm daily subjected. I don't mind answering. I didn't quit teaching until I was seventy-two."

"That's a lot of years."

"You mean that's a lot of years for one teacher to terrorize students devoid of any interest in the development, care, and feeding of the English language."

Kaye couldn't suppress her giggles. "Well, since you put it that way—"

"You graduated with my last full class. I returned the following September for three weeks to substitute for a teacher on maternity leave, and then that was it."

"You must have gone traveling afterwards."

"Why, yes. How did you guess?"

Kaye knew she was breaking all her own rules. She forged on anyway. "Did you go to Europe? Travel to Greece and Rome?"

"I did." Mrs. Gildecott's face took on a puzzled expression.

"You liked the myths so much, Mrs. G. I remember 'cause I took your mythology class. You even talked about the myths in sophomore composition."

"Ah, yes." She nodded and got a faraway look in her eyes. "I was gone for fourteen weeks. I saw all the sights and ate wonderful varieties of food. I folk-danced in Athens and toured the Parthenon and the Coliseum and every other lovely ruin, and I went on to France, Germany, Poland, the United Kingdom. I always wanted to go to Asia and Africa, too. I meant to return one day. Unfortunately, I never made it back overseas, and in my present predicament, I'm unlikely to do so."

Kaye lifted the mop and dunked it into the sudsy water, suddenly overcome with the desire to flee. She rolled the mop bucket toward the door.

"Kaye?"

She didn't meet Mrs. Gildecott's eyes. "Yeah?"

"If I were to pay you for your trouble, would you consider doing a favor for me?"

"It depends on what it is."

"Always the cautious one."

Kaye paused in the doorway and peered out into the hall, waiting. Mrs. Crocker, the wraith, slithered past shrieking, "Help me! Help me! They're after me." Her high, piercing cry faded, and after a few seconds, Kaye turned back to Mrs. Gildecott.

"My dear, the selection of donated books here runs heavily toward light fiction and war books. If I gave you a list of topics, would you stop at the library and check out some books for me?" When Kaye didn't answer immediately, she said, "I would be glad to leave a deposit with you—in case any of the books were damaged or lost."

Rapid clicking of heels on the tiled floor startled Kaye, and she looked out to see Sheila Thornton steaming her way. With a hurried glance back, Kaye said, "I'll think about it," then rolled the mop bucket into the hall.

Kaye entered the Seaton Center juggling a heavy stack of books. She was glad it was Saturday and the weekend staff was on duty. Even better, Sheila Thornton was nowhere in sight.

The pile of books included *The Iliad* by Homer; *Three Plays* by Sophocles; *Till We Have Faces: A Myth Retold* by C.S. Lewis; travel guides to Turkey, Russia, and China; *Outdoor Survival Skills*; *Cold Weather Facts*; and *An Encyclopedia of Country Living*. Kaye thought this a strange combination, but if she were ever cooped up in bed, she'd likely want a variety, too. She had also checked out two additional books she thought Mrs. Gildecott might find interesting: Krakauer's *Into Thin Air* and the biography of aviator Beryl Markham.

When she reached room 18, Mrs. Gildecott said, "Kaye! I didn't expect to see you here today."

Kaye set the books on the end of the bed. "The library was open this morning, so I picked up the books on your list." She dragged a chair from Mrs. Hoffmeier's bedside over next to Mrs. Gildecott.

"I hope it was no trouble at the library." With a groan, she shifted forward and adjusted her bed's incline so she was sitting nearly upright.

"Nope. I told the guy I wanted science, philosophy, and travel literature. No problem. I wasn't sure what editions you wanted of anything, but here's what I got."

"Oh, I'm sure these will all be fine—just fine. Thank you." Mrs. Gildecott leaned forward and pointed. "If you'll get me my purse from that cabinet over there, I'll write you a check."

Kaye shook her head. "That's not necessary. I renewed my library card. As long as we get them back in three weeks, it doesn't cost a thing."

"But for your time and trouble."

"It was really no trouble, and my time is worth next to nothing."

Mrs. Gildecott sighed and sank back. "I think it's high time you and I divulged some personal details. I'm not sure our correctional system does a very good job with rehabilitation. Retribution, yes, but when it comes to restoring one to a level of esteem and faith—well, I think the system fails."

Kaye didn't respond. Once more she had the urge to flee the room.

"What did they do to you in there, Kaye?"

Kaye shifted so her elbows were on her knees and she was staring down at the floor. "How did you know?"

"Know what? That they did something to you?"

"No." She laced her fingers together and stared at them. "That I was in jail."

"I know where a lot of my students went, what they do for a living, if they have achieved successes or disappointments. I know Dennis Creighley became an alderman in Chicago, and Lisle Fredericks married that Hollywood action hero fellow. Did you know Mark Udall—he graduated a year or two ahead of you—was killed in Afghanistan? Such a waste. Missy Peterson writes scripts for one of those daytime shows. When I taught her proper grammar, I had no idea she would be subverting the knowledge for soap operas."

Kaye laughed. "I haven't kept up with any of my classmates."

"Some of them aren't worth keeping up with, my dear, and some have disappeared. But I still get an occasional letter."

Kaye sat back in the hard chair and watched Mrs. Gildecott as she continued to speak of her students. Her eyes sparkled, and her haggard face was transformed to smiling and gleeful, a joy to behold. Mrs. G was nothing like the dragon-queen of high school days. She was someone Kaye wished she had known better long ago.

"—and so all that brings us back to the matter of you."

"What?"

"You. And what you choose to do with your life."

Was this to be the kind of speech Kaye's father delivered with regularity? She bit back disappointment and was reminded why she had rules about consorting with the patients. She tried not to be defensive with her answer. "I don't think you know anything about my life or my choices."

Mrs. Gildecott peered at her with such intensity that Kaye looked away. "There exists a wall inside you from which you recoil. You need to get around or over that wall, and then your life will feel worth living."

"You can tell all this by what—my mopping technique?" Kaye rose and grabbed the back of the chair, ready to return it to its spot near Mrs. Hoffmeier's window.

"There are far more ways to see into the heart of a human being than you can likely comprehend at the moment." Her eyes met Kaye's with conviction. "Please, sit down. I should like to hear about what goes on behind your wall."

As if in a trance, Kaye let go of the back of the chair, stepped around it, and sank into her seat.

"First, can you tell me how you managed to lift such a great sum of money? I suspect that took great cleverness—perhaps something with the checks or deposits? The newspapers never said, and I have always been most curious."

Kaye examined the open face before her. It showed no malice, no accusation. She cleared her throat and softly said, "It wasn't that hard. You'd be surprised how unsafe banks can be. I can assure you, though, no one will ever let me work with money again."

"See? What did I tell you? You're too clever by half, girl!"

In the prior three years, Kaye had never made a friend at Seaton, but Mrs. Gildecott somehow accomplished what no one else had. Whenever Kaye entered room 18, the old woman was usually reading. The last two Saturdays, Kaye had returned books and checked out new requests, always about mythology, philosophy, and natural sciences.

On the Saturday before Christmas, she sat near the foot of Mrs. Gildecott's bed. "You seem so interested in science. Why is that?"

"To be honest, I never paid much attention to the topic, but I have developed a curiosity about certain aspects."

"Did you like the biography of Michelangelo?"

"Yes, a great deal, but not nearly so much as the one about Beryl Markham. Did you know she was the first person to fly solo across the Atlantic from east to west? Not the first woman, the first *person*."

"There are a lot of things I don't know."

"Ah, but you have so many years ahead of you to think and study and learn. Did you like the novel about Joan of Arc?"

"I did," Kaye said. She had liked it a great deal more than she had expected. She'd gotten lost in the narrative, and when the book was finished, she felt bereft and craved more. "I wish there was more. I wish she hadn't had to die at the end. She was too young."

"Yes, any death, regardless of the age, is too young. I shall make a list of books you simply must read, dear. When I'm gone, I do hope you will continue your studies. You have a fine mind and ought to consider attending college sometime soon."

Kaye blushed. She couldn't afford it even if she could figure out a way to get in.

Mrs. Gildecott leaned forward, scrutinizing Kaye's face. "You think that because of your history they wouldn't accept you, but you're wrong, Kaye. Start small and take a course at the community college. I would wager you'll find yourself good at it. You're thorough, as evidenced by your careful work here, and if you would come out from behind that wall and give it a chance, you would be surprised at what you could accomplish."

Mrs. Hoffmeier wheezed and let out a grunt. In a quavering voice, she called out, "Is there to be no peace for me ever? What do I have to do to get a little sleep around here?"

Kaye met Mrs. Gildecott's eyes, and both women stifled their laughter.

"Take me out, Kaye. Get me out of here."

"I don't want to hurt you. I'll call the aides."

"No." She pushed off the bed covers, revealing a pair of pale pink cotton pants that did not go well with the emerald-green top she wore. With a wince, she shifted her right leg until it slipped off the bed. Kaye rose and stood close, helping her to get seated on the edge of the bed with her knuckles white from gripping the mattress. "Just get that wheelchair, will you, dear?"

Kaye rolled it over and locked the wheels. She could tell that balancing on the edge was painful, so she hastily lifted the small woman and settled her in the chair. "Wow, you don't weigh much, Mrs. G."

Through gritted teeth she said, "I seem to be shrinking."

"Are you all right?" Kaye felt a surge of panic. Maybe this wasn't a good idea after all. What if she fell?

"I'm fine." Mrs. Gildecott's face had gone from relaxed and smiling to gaunt and gray.

"Let me get your feet set up." With a few quick motions Kaye adjusted the metal foot supports. "There you go."

"I know this will sound like an unusual request, Kaye, but could you leave me here for a few moments?" She reached for the call cord, then looked back. "Please step out into the hall, and if no one is in sight, could you duck into some other room?"

"What?"

"Please? Please give me a few minutes here to adjust.

Let's say ten minutes."

"All right." Kaye assumed Mrs. Gildecott had suddenly decided she needed to use the toilet, so she left the room and went down the hall to the staff lounge, keyed the code on the door, and slipped inside the empty room.

A four-foot-tall wreath with a plaid bow overwhelmed the wall near the door. Glitter had been spilled on the table in the middle of the room, and someone had decorated above the refrigerator and around the window with clots of hideous, multi-colored lights that blinked erratically. A gangly tree, festooned with tinsel and mismatched bulbs, stood over in the corner. One of the lights on the patient alert panel—one bulb for each of the thirty-six rooms—flashed. Room 6. Mister Rother with the Alzheimer's. By the time someone reached his room, he usually couldn't remember why he had called for assistance.

Kaye was glad she was going to be off work Christmas Eve. The annual staff Christmas party always took place then, and she was happy to miss it. She looked forward to spring. She planned to take a week off and go somewhere warm.

At the pop machine she bought a Pepsi, then sat on one of the two couches and thought about what Mrs. Gildecott had said. Should she consider taking some classes? Kaye liked the idea. Reading escape literature and watching Sci-Fi TV and marathons of "Law and Order" had long ago gotten old. In fact, her whole life felt old. Predictable. Boring. Useless.

She stood up and looked out the window into the ice and snow as she sipped the soda. Small bits of snow blew off the roof and formed a swirl in the gray light. Someone had shoveled the paths, and Kaye had the urge to go out for a smoke. But her cigarettes were in her coat, which hung in Mrs. Gildecott's closet, so she waited.

When enough time had passed, she took a last swig of Pepsi, tossed the can, and made her way back to room 18, almost running into the aide, Susie.

"Brock, what are you doing here?"

"Came by to see Mrs. Gildecott."

Susie lowered her voice. "She's improving. She managed to get herself into a wheelchair all on her own. I'm so happy for the sweet old dear. Maybe she'll get out of here soon."

Kaye heard a squeak and looked to the doorway. Mrs. Gildecott inched forward, her face white as if in pain, as she pushed the wheelchair wheels. She looked up and winced out a wan smile.

Susie reached down and patted Mrs. Gildecott's knee. "Good work, sweetie pie. I wish all the patients had your determination."

"I endeavor always for improvement. Kaye, are you ready for a stroll?"

"Sure. Let me help." She squeezed through the doorway and got behind the chair. "What was that all about?" she whispered into Mrs. Gildecott's ear.

"Shhh, I'll tell you in a bit. Take me out. Take me someplace where we can speak privately."

On Monday morning, the day before Christmas Eve, Kaye stood in the housekeeping closet running water in the utility sink. Her hands shook. This was Day Three of Mrs. Gildecott's campaign, and Kaye was weakening.

Was what Mrs. Gildecott proposed a crime? A sin? How much trouble would Kaye get into, and would she be caught? When was a crime also a mortal sin? And was it forgivable or not?

She ran lukewarm water over her hands, then patted wet palms against heated cheeks. Her face was on fire. She reached for a towel in the stacks on the rack to the left and buried her face in it. Unexpectedly, tears sprang to her eyes. With Mrs. Gildecott gone, Seaton would be a bleak place—even bleaker than it had been before the elderly woman had come to stay—because now Kaye had a taste of companionship, understanding, and human kindness.

How could I expect her to stay on hold, immobile, in pain, waiting for her final demise? Why couldn't I move her to my place to take care of her?

Even as she considered the idea, Kaye realized she not only lacked the resources, but she wasn't there for at least nine hours a day. *Dammit!* she thought bitterly. *Why did I let myself get involved?*

Decisions about what Mrs. Gildecott proposed weren't to be lightly made, and she wished she had someone—anyone—to talk to. But the one person with insight who was trustworthy was Mrs.

Gildecott, and Kaye already knew how she would answer. She wiped her eyes with the towel and fought back the tears.

"Brock." Kaye jerked around to see Marcus looming in the doorway. "Any chance you could work swing shift for me on Christmas Eve?" She stared at him, not answering. "It's double time. I originally switched shifts with Carlos on swing, and now my wife tells me her family has changed our Christmas celebration from the 25th to the 24th. Come on, will ya? I gotta know now. You want the extra hours?"

"Double time?" she squeaked out.

"Yeah. Look, I know it's last minute and all, but I'd really appreciate it if you could cover for me. I'll pay you back somehow in the future."

"Okay."

"You'll do it?"

"Sure."

He grinned, his big teeth wolfish in the dim light. "I owe you, Brock. I'll let Thornton know." He moved away from the doorway.

Was the world conspiring against her? Was this a sign?

"All the books are there on the shelf, Kaye." Mrs. Gildecott pointed toward the half-empty closet. "If you return them within the next two weeks, you'll have them in on time." Kaye accepted this information wordlessly. Mrs. Gildecott lay on her back, pillows propping her up, one book cradled in her hands. She wore a gold and brown paisley brocade vest over a lightweight black turtleneck.

"You look happy, Mrs. G."

"I am. Today I slip the surly bonds of earth, and I am relieved and joyous." She reached out and took Kaye's hand in her firm grip. "Do you think I'm a lunatic?"

"Not like in high school." The words slipped out, and Mrs. Gildecott burst into a delighted laugh that tinkled in the room, echoing over Kaye's head like celestial music. "I didn't mean that."

"I know just what you meant, and you need not worry that I'd misinterpret your honesty. It's wonderfully refreshing. Here, listen." She picked up the book in her lap. "One of the nurses lent me this book, and I was struck by this line: 'Suffering is not the border on the outer edges of one's life, but the cloth itself, elegantly stitched on one side, crude and miserably sewn on the other.' Isn't that lovely?"

"What does it mean?"

"What do you think it means?"

"Suffering is both good and bad?"

"Well . . . yes, but I think it's even more than that. Life is shot through with suffering, but you can decide if you want to focus on the elegant side or the crude, miserably sewn side. Either way, both are there for each person."

Kaye still wasn't sure she understood. "Who wrote that?"

"Alice Hoffman in her novel *Blue Diary*. Here, you should read the book." She set it on the bed's coverlet. "I believe you would enjoy it." She reached under her covers and took out a steno pad. "This is quite messy, but I've written pages and pages of authors and topics you simply must investigate. Study hard. I'll be checking on you."

Kaye fought to keep from crying. She glanced over her shoulder. Seeing and hearing no one coming, she bent over the tiny woman and gently took her in her arms. Now she couldn't hold back the tears. When she let go, Mrs. Gildecott smiled.

"Now, now, dear, no tears." She took Kaye's hand. "Every time you think of me, you must know that it is then I'll be looking in on you."

Kaye's heart beat with such force she could feel it in her arms and legs. For a brief moment, she felt light-headed. "Oh, Mrs. G. I don't know. Are you sure you want to do this?"

Mrs. Gildecott's laugh was rich and full-bodied. "I'm certain. And remember, you're not out from behind those prison walls in your mind until you decide you're truly free. It's up to you." She winked and offered the steno pad. "Go on, take it. And I believe you have something for me?"

In a dull voice, Kaye said, "Three six nine three."

"Thank you. Your friendship has been a joy, Kaye. Now go on with your work. I'll see you when everyone is at the Christmas party. Here's lookin' at you, kid."

Kaye mopped the area around the charge nurse's desk. All afternoon she had been careful to stick close to one aide or another.

Sheila Thornton passed her, pausing to turn and say, "You've certainly been glum all day, Brock. What's the matter—your Christmas tree burn up?"

Kaye stared at the woman. Her exterior was so attractive, so lovely, but the interior was rotten clear through. Why did it have to be this way? Why did good people find themselves in terrible situations without any recourse, without any escape, while nasty people like Sheila Thornton were allowed comfort and beauty and happiness?

When she didn't get a response from Kaye, the administrator made a tsk-tsk sound and walked away. Kaye stared at her back and was suddenly consumed with anger.

The sounds of laughter spilled out of the staff lounge as Thornton opened the door. Kaye stared at the clock over the charge nurse's station. Oh, my. It's after six now—time for the Christmas party.

She pushed the rolling bucket aside, cut through the nurse's station, and hustled down to room 18. Mrs. Gildecott lay in her brocade vest, looking slightly alarmed. "I thought you weren't coming." The clock on her wall read twelve minutes after six.

"Your clock is a little fast." Kaye hesitated, her heart thumping.

"You're worrying again." Mutely, Kaye nodded. "Stop it. You'll not be responsible for my escape."

"Yes, I will."

Mrs. Gildecott laughed. "This is no place for an intelligent person. If one still has her wits about her, she can find out anything she needs to know by guile, and the information I've given my attorney will indicate that. Come now. Help me." As Mrs. Gildecott removed the covers, Kaye maneuvered the wheelchair over and lifted her into it. "Thank you, dear. Try your very best to give me at least an hour head start. Run now. You must not be seen."

At the door Kaye looked back. Mrs. Gildecott raised a hand. "Enjoy life, dear. Enjoy!"

Heart beating fast, Kaye charged out the door, wove her way between three sleeping occupants in wheelchairs, and made it to the charge nurse's counter. She heard footsteps and the low murmur of voices. Panicked, she realized her mop and bucket were on the other side, in the other hall. She ducked down behind the counter, grabbed a wastebasket, and strolled out just as Chief Administrator Vander and two administrative assistants reached the counter.

"Hey, there, it's party time," Vander said. "You're joining us, right?"

"Yes, sir."

"Leave the trash for later and come along."

She set down the metal basket and followed them to the staff lounge where she found the other housekeepers, all the nurses and aides, and several staff who weren't even on duty today.

"Merry Christmas!" someone yelled. A CD player clicked on, and the song, "It's Beginning To Look A Lot Like Christmas," played, the voice happy and smooth. Nurse Judy pressed a mug filled with hot apple cider into Kaye's hand, and she eased her way over next to one of the couches and leaned against the wall.

For the next thirty minutes, awards were given out, people laughed and joked, and everyone helped themselves to plates of holiday sweets. Kaye stood glued to the wall, her heart in her throat. When the light for room 6 flashed, one of the swing shift aides hauled himself up from the couch on the far wall. "Guess I'll go check on Mister Rother. Probably forgot where he put his teeth again."

While he was gone, the light for room 21 flashed. Someone else went to check on that. People came and went, and after a time, Kaye's stress had run so high for so long that she slipped into a sort of dull torpor, unaware of what was happening around her. When she tried to look out the window to the back garden, it was so dark she could see only the reflection of the party.

"Brock."

She came alert with a shock. "What?"

One of the aides said, "Mister Vander just called your name."

Someone else muttered, "She may be dense, but she's always here."

Mister Vander strode across the room and handed Kaye a slip of paper. "Thanks for your reliability. You never missed a day all year."

"You're welcome, sir." She looked down at the Target gift certificate in her hands. Ten dollars. Ten bucks to come to this joyless place where nobody even called her by her first name. She looked around the room. Everybody's last name was stitched into their uniforms, but they were all on first name terms. Only she belonged to a lesser order, the Last Name People.

After a time, the party broke up. Kaye set her mug of untouched cider in the sink and followed Nurse Judy out to the charge nurse's station. Five women hung around there chatting. Kaye picked up her mop and stood nearby, saying nothing, but nodding and listening. She glanced at the clock. Seven p.m.

Kaye stood in the housekeeping closet where she'd spent considerable time all evening removing cans and bags and containers from the shelves, dusting, and wiping down surfaces. The closet was now a disorganized mess. She wasn't sure if rearranging the kitty litter would serve as a good alibi.

At twenty minutes to nine the first shout went up. She stepped into the hallway clutching a dirty cotton rag. Nurse Bradley, who usually worked graveyard, rushed toward her. "Have you seen the resident in room 18—Mrs. Gildecott?"

Kaye shook her head and watched him stride past and head around the corner toward the staff lounge. She returned to the closet and surveyed the wreckage, her hands trembling. At the sink, she ran warm water over her fingers and waited.

The administrators had left long ago, so Kaye was surprised to hear Sheila Thornton's voice in the hallway. "I want every room, every closet, every inch of this entire campus searched. Now!" The voice grew louder, calling out instructions. High heels clicked to a stop in the doorway, and Kaye turned, glad the housekeeping closet was dim.

"Brock, what do you know about this?"

"About what?"

"Where's Esther Gildecott?"

Kaye shrugged. "How should I know?"

Thornton hesitated in the doorway, examining Kaye, then whirled abruptly and moved off. Moments later, Kaye heard the deep bass of one of the male aides calling for help. She followed his shouts toward the back of the facility.

The glass door to the garden was ajar. Gusts of wintry wind blew crystals of snow into the hall. Kaye stepped out and stopped. Her gaze followed parallel lines dug in the snow to the wheelchair glinting silver in the night. Mrs. Gildecott had managed to half turn it and sat in profile near the bare arbor, her elbows on the chair's arms and her palms up as if meditating. Her head was tipped back slightly, her face toward the heavens, with a wisp of a smile gracing ghostly white features.

"Shit," the aide said. "She's frozen solid." He grabbed at the wheelchair and dragged it, his big feet leaving footprints in the carpet of snow.

People pushed past Kaye, shouting, calling out orders. She heard a siren in the distance. Tears poured down her face.

For the first time since her childhood, Kaye had the desire to go to church, to step inside the confessional, and be absolved of her guilt. Were her actions a crime? She was complicit in the death of another human being. How could she ever come to terms with that?

She didn't work Christmas Day and called in sick for the two days following. She stayed up late, smoking, pacing, crying.

On the third day, she went to work. She learned both Sheila Thornton and Vander, the chief administrator, had been reassigned to jobs elsewhere in the nursing home network. The police were still nosing around, asking questions, but it appeared the cause of death would be determined as suicide. The garden door was now boarded over. Nice of them to lock the barn after the horse is through, Kaye thought. At noon there was a memorial service for Mrs. Gildecott, but she couldn't bring herself to attend.

When she arrived home that night, she found an envelope in her mailbox. She stepped inside, opened it, and read a letter written in a shaky hand.

Dear Kaye,

Knowing your propensity for self-blame, I arranged to have my solicitor send this letter to you after my passing. Thank you for all the kindnesses you showed me. You made my final days a joy in ways you might never know, and I am eternally grateful.

I am released now from my prison. Please remember that, as Wittgenstein said, "A man will be imprisoned in a room with a door that's unlocked and opens inwards, as long as it does not occur to him to pull rather than push." You've been pushing far too long. Move on, dear, or I shall haunt you from the grave!

In one year, my solicitor will be contacting you. In the meantime, I hope you will get out of that horrid job and prepare for a new and better life. Consider this a Voice from the grave—or from the Great Unknown—spurring you on to better things. You deserve it, Kaye. Your parole is soon over, and it's time to start living.
Love Always,
Esther Gildecott

P.S. Do not forget to return the library books. And please—visit Greece and Italy some day and think of me.

Kaye wondered if Mrs. Gildecott had suffered. Was there pain? How long did it take? How much courage did it take to do what Mrs. G had done? She still wondered if her part in Mrs. G's death was a crime. But how could it be a sin to do something like that?

"Could I ever be that brave?" she asked aloud. At what point did the balance tip between wanting to live and needing to die?

Kaye had no idea how to answer these questions, but she did know that continuing to live a joyless, hermetically sealed life was

no longer an option. Even in death, Mrs. Gildecott had urged her to live. Maybe it was time for her to do that after all.

"Thank you, Mrs. G," she whispered.

TSUKI, TSUKI

Tee Durant stood between Aisles Three and Four, stacking cans of pineapple rings on the top shelf. She lined them up next to the pears, careful to settle each can just behind the metal lip at the edge of the shelf.

Surrounded by full cartons, she pulled a box cutter from a leather holder on her belt and, with four flicks of the wrist, scored the next carton. She dug strong fingers into the groove and ripped the top off, letting it drop next to her. Cling peaches in heavy syrup. She grabbed cans and moved to the shelf. She didn't much care for overly sweet fruit, but the thought of any kind of food all these hours after breakfast made her stomach grumble. She looked at her watch as she moved back to the box. Nearly seven a.m. She'd been at this for three hours.

"Tee."

"Yeah?" She rose, gripping two fifteen-ounce cans to her chest.

Her boss stood at the end of the aisle, his arms crossed. He wore the same outfit every day: tan shirt and dark brown slacks. The only thing different was the daily tie. He seemed to have six or seven of them. Today's was olive green with some sort of little gold glob every inch.

"Thought you'd be done here."

"I'm close, Mister Hochner."

Hochner gave a nod, then reached for a cigarette tucked behind his ear. "I'm taking a quick ciggy break out back. Watch the clock. If

I'm not back in four minutes, make sure you unlock the door. Mrs. Frahm's been out there in her old tank waiting for the last twenty minutes."

"Will do, boss."

She finished shelving the peaches and sliced open the next box. The tiny individual containers of fruit cocktail took longer to unpack and had to be even more carefully lined up because they tended to lean. Once that box was empty, she kicked it aside. Only Mandarin oranges and applesauce left.

Wiping dusty hands on her green apron, she trotted toward the front entrance.

Candie Butz stood at the register at Checkout One, her hands in the pockets of her dark green smock. With a name like Butz, Tee wondered how she'd ever gotten through junior high school without killing someone. Tee was pretty sure she never would have made it with the name Butz, but maybe things had been different down in Oklahoma where Candie had grown up.

"Hey, Tee," she called out in a slow drawl. "Why not go ahead and let the ol' gal in."

Tee looked through the glass and saw Mrs. Frahm was already nearly to the entrance anyway. Why shouldn't she come on in? She glanced toward the bakery counter over near the manager's office. Genevieve, the older baker, her helmet-shaped hair in an elaborate net, rolled out dough beside Ally, a scrawny woman with stained teeth who never looked calm except when she was out back smoking a cigarette. Ally didn't look up, but Genevieve gazed across the racks of buns and bread, her expression hard.

Tee hesitated, then looked away. Behind the unoccupied service counter, she entered the code to turn on the automatic door. The wind blew Mrs. Frahm's short silver hair up off one side of her head. Her pink and purple muumuu billowed in the summer breeze as she stepped on the pad. The door slid open, and she steamed in, dropped a purse as big as a suitcase into the metal basket, and shoved off like a tugboat dragging a wheezing pastel-colored barge. Tee glanced over at Candie, who smiled and shrugged.

Tee hustled back to her final two cartons. She went down on one knee with the box cutter just as Parker Feeney came strolling down the aisle, hands in his jeans pockets. The front of his green apron was spotless, and his white Nikes appeared brand-new. Just out of high school, he was working the seven-to-three shift at Hochner's until college started in the fall.

"Tee, Tee, Tee." As he drew near, he leaned down and in a low voice said, "Perfect place for you—the fruit aisle." With a snicker he waltzed past, leaving the smell of sickly-sweet aftershave behind him.

Her face burned. She despised Parker Feeney. He was a cocky, rude, know-it-all who never missed a chance to hassle her. He was like all the verbal bullies she'd ever known—expert at slipping in the jab when no one was looking. She didn't dare hit back, though. Guys like him had a way of coming out looking wronged and wounded while women like Tee got smeared. Mostly she tried her best to ignore him.

Still unsettled, she leaned down and grabbed at a jar of applesauce, but as she brought it up, the container slipped. With the other hand, she grabbed frantically. She swore her heart skipped a beat as she pulled it safely to her chest. "Oh, man," she whispered, relief coursing through her. Glass and apple and slick juice were no fun to clean up. Letting out a sigh, she got a good hold on the glass container and placed it on the shelf.

"Pretty impressive dexterity there."

Tee turned to meet the eyes of a smiling woman in a long-sleeved, pale blue T-shirt and skintight black biking shorts. The brow of her light brown face was speckled with perspiration. She held a bicycle helmet in one gloved hand and ran the other hand through her short Afro. Before Tee could swallow away whatever canned good seemed to have lodged in her throat, the woman went on. "Got any Gatorade?"

Tee cleared her throat. "Sure. Aisle Two. Just around the corner from here." She gestured to the other side of the canned goods aisle.

Parker chose that moment to reappear. "Help you, ma'am?" he asked.

Tee watched as the biking chick glanced at him. As soon as he got a look at her browned, muscular legs and attractive smile, he squared his shoulders and sucked in his stomach. Any second Tee expected him to let out a roar and start beating his chest like King Kong.

"I'm good," the woman said. She turned back to Tee and was about to say something when a gravelly voice behind Tee called out, "Excuse me?"

Mrs. Frahm stood on the other side of the pile of cardboard cartons pushing at her cart's handgrip as though she were revving it up for the Indy 500.

When Tee stood back up from sweeping the empty boxes aside, both the cyclist and Parker Feeney were gone.

Tee's shift ended at noon. She folded up her apron and stuck it in the dinky locker assigned to her. Each of the twenty lockable enclosures was bigger than a breadbox, but not by much. During the winter she could hardly get her coat in, much less her boots. Mostly she used it for spare change, her book, and her apron. Unlike Candie and the other checkers, she didn't need anywhere to lock up her purse. She kept her wallet Velcroed in the cargo pocket at her thigh. If she had any trouble, she could live without her book and vending machine change, but she didn't want to have to come back for a purse.

She retrieved the latest Jane Fletcher adventure she was reading and locked up. As she turned to leave, Parker Feeney and Trey Anderson came through the doorway into the employee area. Trey had an iPod tucked into his shirt pocket. She could hear the music from across the room, even over his humming.

As Trey flopped into one of the four chairs at the break table, Parker leaned down and elbowed his shoulder. Trey bellowed, "What?"

Parker leered at Tee and grinned knowingly. Trey looked up at him, obviously confused. Parker gritted his teeth and snatched one of the plugs from Trey's ear.

"Hey! Gimme back my earphone."

Tee took Trey's momentary outburst as a chance to sidle past Parker, but he let go of the iPod cord and stepped into her path. She knew enough not to back down from him. He only intensified his harassment then. She looked into his blue eyes. His hair was blond, but his eyelashes were long and dark—as beautiful as a woman's. He had every advantage, she thought.

He smiled, years of orthodontia revealing perfect white teeth that must have cost his folks thousands. "You know, butch, you give new meaning to the word butch."

She was his height, about five-eight, but his frame was bigger, his shoulders broader. He was soft though. Tee could see he'd never been a brawler, probably never had a fistfight. She thought she could take him, but he wasn't worth it. "Out of my way, pretty boy."

He smirked and nodded. "Bet I'm not the kind of pretty you're interested in." His tone was so juvenile she expected him to break out in "nyah nyah nyah" next.

She crossed her arms, counted to ten.

He took a piece of bubblegum from his pocket, untwisted the ends, and stuck it in his mouth, a derisive grin on his face the whole time. He chewed noisily, then said, "I saw you looking at that fox earlier. I got you figured out. I think I'll ask her to go on a date with me."

Tee laughed loud.

Parker's face reddened, and he looked uncertain.

She glanced at Trey. He stared up at them with a frown. She leaned down and pretended to speak.

"What?" he said loudly. He pulled out an earplug. "What?"

"I said, your buddy here just told me to stay away from you since you're his boy toy."

"What!" Trey shot up out of the chair, knocking it over behind him. He stepped back, giving Tee just enough room to elbow between the two young men and escape out the door.

The last thing she heard was Parker whispering, "Dyke, dyke, dyke, dyke . . ."

She stomped toward the rear entrance, passing Genevieve along the way. Genevieve wasn't wearing a hairnet, so her bouffant hairdo drew Tee's gaze away from her face, but she still noticed the woman's hard, cold eyes.

"Excuse me." Tee stepped around her and blasted out the rear door.

Her breath came in short bursts. She paced to get herself under control. What she really wanted to do was rearrange Parker's loser face. She could visualize the karate moves so clearly: *maeh geri, oi zuki, empi, tsuki tsuki tsuki*—snap kick, step-in punch, elbow to his middle, punch to the nose, to the ear, under the jaw—and he'd be down for a lot longer than an eight count. He wouldn't be so pretty then, nor would he know whether to cradle his face first or his balls.

But she'd been through that act before, and she recalled quite clearly how badly it had ended.

Violence wasn't the answer. Her *dojo* master had said repeatedly that one who lives her life in accordance with the precepts of karate never attacks first; those who practice karate must follow the way of justice and virtue. But Tee wasn't living in a just world. And she wasn't feeling very virtuous.

Tee did the best she could to avoid Parker Feeney, but he never quit with his patter, a smile on his face while making rude comments *sotto voce* so only she heard them.

Tee liked the job. For now. Hochner's was smaller than the supermarket she'd worked at in Dickinson, North Dakota, and didn't pay as well. But to her advantage, nobody here in Alafair, Minnesota, knew much about her.

Back in North Dakota, she'd met Penny, a nice woman who was a student at Dickinson State University. One day, Penny had come by to pick up Tee after work. She'd leaned on the counter, flirting outrageously, curling her long blonde hair around one finger and making eyes at Tee. Amused and tantalized, Tee engaged in the equivalent of visual footsie while she waited on customers in the eight-items-or-less line.

Tee barely remembered the cowboy type who'd come through her checkout lane.

Ten minutes later, she was off duty, and she and Penny were heading out into the icy winter night. Tee was almost to the passenger side of the F-150 when the cowboy caught up with Penny on the other side.

"Listen, bitch." His voice was deep and raspy.

Penny whirled and let out a gasp of fear. Tee heard the tinkle of metal on concrete and knew Penny had dropped her keys.

"Hey, you asshole," Tee shouted. "Get away!" She ran to the rear of the truck.

Penny stumbled back, the man talking a streak of trash.

Tee stepped in front of Penny and shoved him. He slipped and nearly fell on the icy ground. When he regained his balance, his eyes narrowed, and his face turned red with rage. Cowboy boots, jeans, and a tan workman's jacket. He outweighed her, and was taller, would be even without the boots. She didn't want to tangle with him.

"Get the hell away from us. Back off, and this is over."

"You bitch. You'll pay." He cupped his fist in the palm of his hand and took a half step.

It was his smirk that did her in. She didn't wait for him to take a swing.

Maeh geri, oi zuki, empi, tsuki tsuki tsuki. Blood rushed in her head. She heard the words *tsuki, tsuki, tsuki,* over and over like a chant, the combination of blows as natural as a dance.

He fell between Penny's truck and a van.

She leaned over him, her fist flashing in the pale slice of light from the fluorescent bulb nearby. She smelled his liquor breath and heard a whooshing sound, repeatedly, like a pneumatic piston. Her hand hurt, burning like nettles in her knuckles

Someone pulled her off him.

That's how the night manager found them: the "innocent" cowboy on the ground, Penny scrabbling around on hands and knees in search of her keys, and Tee held from behind by a burly truck driver.

The rage drained away and left her shaking. Blood covered the skinned knuckles on both her hands.

Her head had smacked against the side of Penny's pickup when the trucker grabbed her, and that was her saving grace.

She was arrested for assault and battery, but the goose egg that welled up on her temple and brow belied the cowboy's statement that he'd never hit her.

Still, she spent a sleepless night in jail before the cowboy, one Fritz Volker, a card-carrying member of the American Nazi Party, decided not to press charges. Clearly, he didn't want his Aryan buddies to learn that a 155-pound woman had kicked the crap out of him.

Exhausted, she went home, slept for three hours, soaked her hands in ice, and went to work on time.

Her boss was waiting for her near the service counter. "You can't beat up customers in the parking lot," he said.

The checkers were craning their necks, and two of the stockers had crept up to the ends of aisles to listen. Even some of the customers were watching curiously.

"I was attacked by *him*, Mister Franklin. *He* threatened *us*."

Franklin bit his lip and shook his head slowly. "That may be. But you can't screw around with customers in the store either." He cleared his throat. "'Specially not the lady folk. I paid you for the whole week. Clean out your locker and get out."

Face burning, Tee hustled through the store, back to the employee lounge. Into a grocery bag she stuffed four well-thumbed paperbacks, a sweatshirt, and a blue and white Dickinson Blue Hawks mug Penny had given her. When she attempted to exit through the rear door, Franklin was waiting. He insisted on looking in the bag to make sure she wasn't taking anything that wasn't hers. Then instead of letting her go out the back, he said, "You go on through the store, now. Through the front. You bear your shame instead of slinking out like a coward."

He didn't say it in a mean voice. His tone was so matter of fact that she stared a moment to make sure he was serious. But when she stepped toward the back hallway, he moved in front of her, jaw tensed, and with a toss of his head said, "That way."

Her former coworkers stared, but not one would look her in the eye. She put her head down and raced out the door to her old beater of a car.

When she arrived home, there were messages on the machine from her father and her older brother's wife. They'd somehow heard what had happened—although they seemed to think she had been arrested for fornicating in the parking lot, not fighting. It might have been amusing, except both of them informed her she was no longer welcome in their homes. Not for Thanksgiving, not for Christmas, not for any reason. No amount of calling or explaining got her anywhere. After she made several tries, her family merely hung up whenever she called.

She dialed Penny, who said, "After seeing you go crazy like that, I could never trust you wouldn't beat me. I'll be changing my phone number."

Then she hung up.

Tee sat in her bedroom for three days before the reality of what happened finally set in. She was alone. No job, a bad reputation, and little savings. She didn't even want to go back to the *dojo* and see her karate *sensei*.

So she fled.

Her junker car took her a little over five-hundred miles before the engine blew. She ended up in the YWCA in downtown Saint Paul. They found her a job at Hochner's in Alafair, a small town east of the Twin Cities. She rented a temporary room over the nearby bakery and settled in.

That had been seven months earlier. Since then, she'd found a three-room apartment on Main Street above the coffee shop, and she'd passed her six-month probation at work. But Parker Feeney was testing her, and it ate at her that there was nothing she could do except keep taking his abuse.

Tee was stretched out on her couch, a pillow behind her head and her novel propped up on her stomach, when Mister Hochner called. He had never called her at home. Her mouth went dry, and her stomach cramped.

"Sorry to bother you on your day off, but I was wondering if you might be available to work some extra hours? Candie's swamped, and I need someone to help her at the checkout, run after carts, you know, coordinate every little disaster. I've been here since five. I'd like an hour or two to go home and eat."

"No problem at all, Mister Hochner. It'll take me about fifteen minutes to get there."

She dressed quickly and walked the eight blocks to the store, thankful that although the humidity was intense, it was only in the low eighties. Still, she'd be glad to get into the air-conditioned store.

Cutting between cars, she watched a bicyclist roll into the lot and dismount. She was removing her helmet as Tee approached the front door.

"Hey, it's you," the woman called out.

"Uh, hello. How're you doing?"

"Good, thanks." She smiled, and Tee was struck by how luminous she was, how thoroughly happy the woman looked. Her eyes sparkled clear and dark.

"Beautiful day out. The path around the reservoir was lovely—all those flowers blooming and the water rippling."

Tee came to a stop near the bike's handlebars and watched her lock it up. "Nice bike. I ought to get one."

"You should." She stripped her glove off and stuck out her right hand. "Mona Trask. Call me Moe."

Her hand was firm and warm, and Tee stumbled over her own introduction.

"Tee? Short for Theresa?"

"Tessa."

"Ahh. The nickname suits you." She let go of Tee's hand and removed her other glove. "It'll be nice to pop into the air conditioning. Damn, it's muggy out here."

Tee followed her through the automatic door. A yellow muscle shirt and black biker shorts accentuated Moe's lean physique. Guiltily, Tee looked around, worried someone might notice she was ogling this woman's well-toned assets.

Moe walked past the carts, turned, and stopped. "I didn't see you here last Sunday. I thought maybe you'd quit."

"No. I don't usually work Sundays. Got called in today because we're shorthanded."

"Lucky for me." Moe smiled, her teeth white and even. She gestured with her free hand, and Tee saw a jagged scar on her right biceps. Moe looked down. "Bad car accident, but it's old. Doesn't bug me anymore. So, hey, how about going bike riding sometime?"

"Like I said, I don't have a bike."

"Since I have three, I think you're covered."

"Three?"

"One's a racing bike, and I never sold my old road bike when I got the city model. You could ride that."

Tee hardly knew how to respond. Why in the world would this lovely woman chat with her much less loan her a bike?

She must have looked confused, because Moe bit back a smile and said, "I'm probably being overly forward, aren't I. Maybe we ought to meet for coffee first?"

Glenn Hochner was fast approaching up the cereal aisle. "That's my boss, Moe. I gotta go."

"What's your number?"

Tee recited it, realizing she hadn't given a woman her phone number in more than a year. "I'll write it down."

"Don't worry." Moe pointed to her forehead and grinned. "Steel-trap memory. Besides, I can always stop by during the week if I forget." She backed up saying, "Later, gator," and scooted down the canned goods aisle before Mister Hochner arrived.

"Tee. Thanks for coming in. You're a lifesaver. First order of business is checkout. Could you go help Candie, then spell her for a break when things calm down?"

The checkout line was backed up all the way to the coffee aisle with six carts stuffed full of groceries.

Candie caught sight of her. "Oh, Tee. Thank God. I can't scan and bag fast enough."

"Want me to open a lane? Or bag for you?"

"I can really fly if you'll bag."

Someone in line grumbled, "Open up another damn lane." He was a gray-haired man with a boxer's mashed nose. He held a ham under one arm and a carry-basket full of hot dogs, cold cuts, and Jimmy Dean sausage.

Candie flashed a smile at the heavyset man. "We'll speed up now, hon. Just watch. I'll be with you fast as a cheetah with a hotfoot."

The man's face went from cranky to questioning. "Cheetah with a hotfoot? That's an old Johnny Cash line. You a Johnny Cash fan?"

Tee swept past Candie, grabbed a plastic bag, and packed three heads of lettuce and a cucumber as Candie said, "Why, yes. Momma loved June, but Daddy lived by Johnny Cash. He always said Johnny was an honest man—didn't never lie."

"Well, that's true," the man said, a pleased expression on his face.

Tee glanced around, and the line of people had settled down, everyone listening in on the conversation. She marveled at how Candie could do that. Maybe it was her southern accent or deft multi-tasking. Whatever gift it was, Tee wished she had it.

She was glad when the rush finally cleared and there was a lull. "You know, Candie, you're really so good with the customers. I couldn't do what you do."

Candie straightened her smock and twisted a blonde curl around her index finger. "It wouldn't be modest if I admitted I was tickled to hear that. I just try to get along and be sociable. My daddy always said I was as appealing as apple pie à la mode."

"He must have been a real character."

"Truth is, I never was sure if that was a compliment or he was saying I was too fat." She squared her shoulders and snickered, her breasts rising as she turned a little to the side and struck a pose that fashion models usually avoided.

When she snickered, Tee stammered, "That can't be right. You're not fat at all. You're perfectly propor—" She caught herself before her eyes could sweep the checker's full figure. Once more she was blushing. "I mean, well, you know what I mean. He had to have meant you were appealing or, or—oh, hell."

Candie laughed out loud. "You're sweet, Tee. I think that's about the most I've ever heard you say. And all in defense of little ol' me. I'll tell my boyfriend I've got a protector here. He's always fretting someone will come in and sweep me off my feet. I tell him he's the only one can lift me."

Tee had seen Candie's boyfriend. He had to be at least six-and-a-half-feet tall. Between his height and Candie's voluptuous physique, any kids they had were either going to be pro basketball players or defensive linemen.

"You want me to cover so you can have a break?"

"Please." Candie bent to scoop her purse from under the counter. "My dogs are barking something fierce, and I'd love to take five and rest."

After Candie left, Tee busied herself with refilling the bag dispensers at all the registers. A kid came by with a handful of candy bars, and she rang him up, then she got out paper towels and a spray bottle and wiped down all six checkout stands and counters. She thought about the woman, Moe, and wondered if she'd call.

"Psssst."

Tee looked up from the spilled coffee grounds she was sweeping to see Parker Feeney peering around the Seattle's Best coffee grinder and display.

Before he had a chance to say anything, Genevieve and Ally came down the aisle in their short-sleeved white baker's smocks. Both had flour dusted on their arms. Ally abruptly stopped speaking and looked down. Genevieve frowned. "Parker."

"Yes, ma'am." He turned on a hundred-watt smile.

"Could you bring some more flour bags up while we're on break?"

"No problem, Genevieve. Anything else?"

"Nope." The bakers swept past, leaving behind a scent of cinnamon and almonds. "Four bags will be sufficient," Genevieve said in a low voice.

Tee resumed her sweeping. When the two women disappeared into the storeroom, Parker said, "The skinny one looks like your type. Bet you're hot for those meth teeth."

"Don't you have some work to do? Bales to tote, flour to haul?"

He stepped closer, a menacing look on his face. Tee tightened her grip on the broom and brought it up in front of her. "You come any nearer and you'll find this broomstick whacking you upside the head."

"Oooh, how butch of you. You got a whip and chains to go with your little broom?"

Tee turned away and ignored him until he finally meandered off. As she swept the last of the dirt and coffee into the dustpan, she realized that although Parker's comments were offensive and irritating, they were having less effect than they had at first. Only six or seven more weeks, and then he'd go off to college. But what if he continued to work at Hochner's on breaks and next summer? She liked Hochner's, but she couldn't take Parker's crap forever.

In her tiny galley kitchen, Tee stood trying to decide what to make for dinner. The window air conditioner valiantly attempted to cool the apartment, but the air remained stuffy and warm, too hot to have the oven on. "Microwave dinner it is," she mumbled, but before she could open the freezer door, the phone rang.

"Moe Trask here, Tee. Feel up to a cup of coffee later on?"

"I feel up to a whole dinner right now. Have you eaten?"

"It's been too hot. Haven't been hungry at all," Moe said.

"Maybe if we went somewhere cool?"

"I'll go for that. Burgers? Steaks? Pizza? Vegetarian?"

"Hmmm . . . Pizza?"

"All right." They settled on the pizzeria closest to Tee's apartment, and she was out the door before it even registered that she was meeting a woman she hardly knew. By the time she'd walked the three blocks, she was sweating and nervous.

She expected Moe to be waiting in the comfortably chilled restaurant, so she was surprised to find her leaning against the hot bricks outside next to the bicycle rack. "You rode your bike? I don't know why I expected you to drive here."

Moe laughed. "I called you on my cell from the reservoir. I've been out riding this afternoon."

"You're a braver woman than I am, that's for sure. I've been holed up in my stuffy apartment."

"You're a *smarter* woman than I am, that's all. I actually feel faint from the humidity."

"Let's get inside. You probably need a quart of water." Tee reached for the door and held it open. As Moe squeezed past, Tee couldn't believe how easily they were conversing. It felt natural—as though she'd known Moe far longer than the approximately eight total minutes they'd spent in one another's company at the store.

They found a booth and immediately ordered a pitcher of lemonade. Moe said, "You haven't lived in Alafair long, have you?" Tee shook her head. "I didn't think so. I definitely would have noticed if you had. I've lived here since my senior year in college."

"The U of M?"

"Yup. Accounting and business degree. Now I work as an accountant for 3M. Big bucks, big bore. I should have taken up bicycle sales and repair. I enjoy tinkering a lot more than toting up accounts, but there isn't much money in it."

They talked for two hours, first over pizza, then, after the lemonade was gone, over frosty bottles of St. Pauli beer. Despite the food in her stomach, Tee felt a little buzzed, and she wasn't sure if it was from the beer or company. She hoped she wasn't grinning like an idiot as she listened to Moe talk about "Minnesota Nice" and how everyone treated her respectfully, but with such an air of reserve.

"Racial prejudice?" Tee asked.

"Must be. I'm not sure they tumble on to my lesbian orientation too quickly."

Tee couldn't help but grin. She took another swig of beer and wiped the back of her hand across her mouth. "They tumble on to mine far too fast." There, now it was out.

"I imagine." Moe reached across the table and patted Tee's forearm. "You're a very handsome woman." She said it earnestly, with not a trace of seduction in her voice. "You know that, right?"

Tee felt herself blushing all the way to the roots of her hair. She set down her empty beer bottle and tried to think what to say. No words came.

Moe removed her hand and let out a big sigh. "There I go again, being too forward. My grandma always said, 'Mona's shot through with gobs of gumption.' Guess she was right."

"I like that about you," Tee said shyly.

"You do, do you?" Moe smiled, then checked her watch. "It's still early. Want to hit the nine o'clock movie?"

Still a little buzzed, Tee looked at her in amazement. "Why me?"

"Well, darlin', why not?"

The next two days at the store passed in a blur. As Tee hustled to shelve goods, work the checkout stand, and back up the baggers, Moe was all she could think of: the warm smile, her snapping near-black eyes, the tight Afro which felt so soft in Tee's hands when she kissed her goodnight after the movies.

She'd been so high on movie M&Ms and Moe's presence that she'd forgotten to get Moe's phone number, but Moe had called her yesterday and come by the store this morning. They were going out for pasta after Moe got off work. Tee kicked empty boxes out of the way and hastened to get the last of the Chef Boyardee Beefaroni on the shelf.

"Tee. You can't say I'm not a quick study. I've learned some new words for you."

"Oh, shit," Tee muttered under her breath as she watched Parker approach. "I don't want to hear them." She pushed the cart down the aisle, but he caught up with her.

"Carpet muncher," he whispered. This set him off into gales of laughter.

Trey came out of the back room, adjusting his green apron. Parker hastened over and blocked Tee from pushing the flat cart through the double doors.

"Trey, Trey. Get a load of the muff diver."

To his credit, Trey gave Parker a scowl. "Jesus. What's your deal? Move. I need to get to work." He pushed past, got to the paper goods aisle, and stepped aside for Genevieve and Ally.

Genevieve glared at Tee. "You oughtn't let that boy talk to you like that." Her lips were turned down in a disapproving frown. Tee stood, mouth open. As if she had any control over Parker's malicious mouth. She watched helplessly as Genevieve and Ally disappeared into the back room.

"That's it," she said. "I've had enough of you."

He laughed.

Tee closed her eyes for a moment, envisioning the combination of *oi zuki, tsuki, oi zuki, tsuki tsuki tsuki*—step-in punch, strike to the middle, step back, strike the nose, the ear, under the jaw.

She opened her eyes. He stood waiting, expectant, almost as if he wanted her to attack. She couldn't understand him in the slightest.

"You don't exist, Parker Feeney. You hear me? You're dead to me." To prove her point, she grabbed the handle and shoved the flat cart toward the double doors, forcing him to scramble to get out of the way.

Once she'd parked the cart, Tee headed back, passing the break room where she saw Genevieve and Ally carrying on a whispered conversation. Genevieve was pointing an index finger in the air. Ally sat looking frightened, her brown eyes wide and her face pale. Tee kept going. She walked along the salty snacks row and paused to straighten up the Olde Dutch Potato Chip section.

When she got to the front registers, Parker was bagging for a checker named Sondra. Candie caught her eye. "Tee, you have a little time? Can you spell Ronnie? He'd like a break."

Tee grabbed a paper bag and shook it open. When Parker Feeney looked over his shoulder, his handsome features sly and twisted, she looked right past him.

"So this little asshole is basically sexually harassing you." Moe made it a statement, not a question.

"Pretty much." Tee sipped a Sloe Gin Fizz. The first swigs had gone straight to her head, so she was proceeding cautiously until their food arrived.

Moe had slugged down half of her drink already, and now she spun the glass in her long fingers. "And he's only eighteen? Sucks. Totally sucks. What are you going to do?"

"I can't decide whether I should kick his ass or quit."

"Not the latter. Definitely not that."

"Most of the time I work hard at imagining he doesn't exist."

"If you have to imagine something doesn't exist, then doesn't it exist?"

Tee let out a sigh. "Yeah, I suppose you're right. I should just call him out back and let him have it."

"But he's bigger than you. I could show you some moves so you could drop him before he could get at you."

"I know enough karate to kill him, Moe."

"Really? How come I never see you at the *dojo*?"

Tee sputtered into her drink. Moe was full of surprises. "There's a *dojo* here in town?"

"Of course. Not many women, but enough for a women's session Saturday mornings after the little kids. The rest of the time the men tend to hog the place, but I go on Tuesday and Thursday most weeks."

"Today's Thursday."

"I know." She smiled. "I preferred having dinner with you. But this is great news! Now you can join the *dojo*, and we can spar together."

"Oh, I don't know." The thought of sparring with Moe, harming her in any way, shook up Tee in a way she couldn't explain. "It'd be too easy to hurt you."

"So you're a black belt?"

Tee shook her head. "Brown belt—two black bars. Just reached that level before I left Dickinson."

A smirk graced Moe's face, and she looked so pretty it took Tee's breath away. "Bad news for you, girlfriend. I've had a black belt since I turned twenty-one. I'll try hard not to hurt *you*. How about I get my *bo* and *bakken*, and the two of us track down this little jerk and kick his ass."

Tee looked at Moe, really studied her. "Are you serious?

You've got karate staffs and wooden swords?"

"Nah, but I could get some from the *sensei* if you want me to. I've found a regular old stick works quite effectively."

"What?"

"I've got three older brothers. I had to learn self-defense early, and believe me, I used any weapon at hand—spatula, croquet mallet, fly swatter. I was turning into such a violent child that my dad put us all in training. I started karate at eight."

"Wow."

Moe slid her Rum Collins across the table. "Taste this. Does it seem a little funky to you?"

The rum burned going down, and the slice of orange stuck to the side of the glass fell off and splatted on the table. Tee sputtered and choked. "Oops."

Moe laughed. "It is funky, isn't it?"

"I think they forgot some of the soda."

On Day Ten of dating Moe, Tee was as certain as she'd ever been that she was in love. She had no clue how these feelings had crept up on her so quickly, but she'd never had so much fun with anybody in her life. Moe made her laugh, and already Tee felt a fierce protectiveness for her, which Moe seemed to feel for Tee as well. Moe kept telling her she'd be glad to help Tee confront her nemesis, but Parker Feeney didn't seem worth one minute of Moe's time.

Tee had begun looking in the classifieds for new jobs, but she hated to quit. Her boss had recently given her a dollar an hour raise. She was trusted, and though both of the bakers, some of the box boys, and one of the cashiers treated her coolly, everyone else was polite.

Then on a Monday night in early August, Hochner called a meeting of the entire staff. In an unusual move, all three of the shift supervisors had been called in to cover customer service and the checkout lanes so every staff member could attend. Before the meeting, Candie pulled Tee aside. "What's up? You have any idea?"

Tee shrugged. "Haven't got a clue."

"Something's been going on for days. Mister H has been stomping around, upset, and I've seen some of the box boys in and out of his office."

Now that Candie mentioned it, Tee had noticed people were extra cranky, but she'd been so busy she hadn't paid any attention. "You think there's money trouble? The store's not closing?"

"I doubt that. Old Man Hochner left this place paid off, and his son's as big a tightwad as he was. No," Candie said, "it's something else." She took Tee's arm. "Come on, let's go get a good seat."

It felt odd, but sort of good, to be ushered down Aisle Twelve by the blonde cashier. Candie kept up a running commentary all the way, and, when they got to the storeroom, the box boys had cleared out an area and set up four rows of folding chairs. Candie headed for the rear corner, exactly where Tee preferred.

Soon the room was full. Glenn Hochner entered followed by a man and woman dressed in neat, professional suits. Mister Hochner raised a hand, and the black tie he wore slipped askew. "People. Give me your attention, please."

Genevieve and Ally sat a row ahead and to the far right. Seated and in profile, Genevieve looked less angry, her face relaxed, and her dark blonde hair not so tightly helmeted. She glanced Tee's way, amazing Tee with a brief smile. It changed the entire cast of her face.

But before Tee could get over the transformation, Mister Hochner said, "We have a problem here, and it needs to be dealt with. In this store, on these grounds, we respect one another. We help one another. We work as a team. We've been a family store since 1921, and we will continue to be so for as long as it's called Hochner's."

A murmur of agreement rose from the group.

"My father taught me to address problems head on and get help where needed. These folks, Mary Trimble and Daniel Staples, are here to talk to all of you about sexual harassment. We'll be having an overview tonight, and then they'll speak to you in small groups over the next few weeks. I hold you all to high standards, and I'd appreciate it if you'd listen closely."

There was a flurry of motion to Tee's right, and Genevieve rose.

"Yes, Gen? What is it?" Mister Hochner asked.

"Many of you know about me and my partner, Eileen, and most of you are very respectful. But I've put up with some harassment for a while, and I don't want it to happen anymore. You respect me, I'll respect you."

Tee's mouth went dry, and she was so shocked by what she'd heard that she sat for a moment not breathing. Genevieve sat down with a whumping sound, then glanced back over her shoulder, one eyebrow raised.

"Uh, yes, thank you, Genevieve. Anyone else?" Hochner's eyes came to rest on Tee, and he looked at her expectantly. She didn't move, so he said, "Okay, let me turn it over to Mary and Daniel."

Tee's gaze swept the room, looking for Parker Feeney, but he was nowhere to be seen. Had she gotten so used to pretending he didn't matter that he had actually ceased to exist? She elbowed Candie and whispered, "Where's Parker?"

Candie turned and looked at Tee for a long moment. "Whoa, doggies," she said, her voice filled with wonderment. "He stomped out of Mister H's office a couple days ago, and I didn't think much of it, but you know what? I think he got fired. Deserved it, too. Foul-mouthed little bastard."

Tee couldn't help but grin. "That'd be my lucky day."

She looked around at the women in the room, suddenly realizing perhaps she hadn't been the only woman he said rude things to. Maybe she should have talked to people.

Two hours later, Tee dialed Moe's house. "You'll never believe this. Guess whose ass got fired?"

"Oh, hon," Moe said, "please tell me not yours?"

"No way. Parker Feeney. He's gone. And you won't believe how this went down."

Moe let out a squeal. "So we don't have to kick his ass after all?"

"Nope. Not this time."

"But we're ready if we ever have to, right, hon?"

Tee shook her head and clutched the phone. Such warm feelings ran through her that for a moment she didn't know what to say. She thought of Genevieve and Ally, a couple of odd ducks. She hadn't given them a chance, but she now believed she'd make an effort to get to know them. She had a friendship blossoming with Candie, and to top that off, Glenn Hochner was a decent man. Maybe sometimes there was justice in the world. And it didn't have to come from the end of her fist.

Sounding breathless, Moe said, "You have to tell me all about it."

"Gladly. I'm off work now."

"Good. Come to my house, why don't you. Oh, and Tee?"

"Yeah?"

"Bring your toothbrush."

ANOTHER STAGE

"I don't believe in soul mates."

That was the last logical comment Brianna made as she packed to move out. Ash Tarrant was stunned into silence with that one. Then again, Brianna had never believed in anything unless it benefited her.

Ash went into the living room and sank down on the couch, exhausted. Maybe it's better she's going, Ash thought. She sure wasn't much good to me while I was in the hospital. If that couldn't make her into a soul mate . . .

Four hours later, Brianna carted out the last of her things (and a good deal of Ash's) to Rita's Dodge Ram pickup. Rita was on their softball team—a friend, Ash had thought. Not anymore. Brianna was subtle as a brick to the side of the head, and Rita had fallen for her hard. Rita, late twenties going on fifteen, was blonde, shapely, a bubble-headed lesbian Barbie who wouldn't stand much storm from Brianna. Like most women—Ash included—Rita would walk the plank for Brianna, and when Brianna was done with her, little Rita would find herself attached to a nice big chunk of cement block and sent to the depths.

On her final pass through the front door, Brianna turned and looked at Ash, her light brown hair knotted into a mess and her green eyes wet with tears. "Why'd you have to go and do that to yourself, Ash? Why?"

"It was surgery or die."

"You don't know that. You could have had radiation or something." She sobbed dramatically. "Instead, look what you've done to yourself."

"Yeah, yeah, now I'm only half a woman. Get the hell out. You've got the sensitivity of a pig." That was probably an insult to pigs, but Ash was so shocked and hurt she couldn't think of anything else to say.

I can live without a breast, but I'd be damned if I'd die at age forty—even if it meant having two perfect tits.

And given what had just happened, apparently she could live without a soul mate, too.

Two months after the surgery, the incision had gone from a raging red slice to a deep, dark purple line, and all around it—for a good two to three inches—she had no feeling. She feared she had serious nerve damage, but the doctor told her feeling would gradually come back, that the skin would once again come to life.

Ash tried not to look at the scar. Six inches of anguish was how she thought of it. She'd glance at her chest in the mirror every once in a while. She could see the little dots on either side of the wound, all the places where staples had held the raw edges together.

Zipper-Tit.

If she'd had someone to share it with, the morgue humor would have lightened her mood.

By the four-month mark, she wished she had someone to show that the scar had gone from a horrid purple to a lighter fuchsia color. She could still see those tiny dots, but was it her imagination—hadn't they faded a lot? She wished she had someone to ask.

When Brianna left, she seemed to have taken their mutual friends with her—and the couples weren't comfortable with Ash alone anyway. What a shock it had been with everyone paired off. Two by two by two.

She contemplated moving back to Duluth, but decided she needed to go it alone for a while. Though her three brothers were sympathetic, they weren't much help.

Ash ran Tarrant Tuneworks, a professional recording studio for musicians in the Twin Cities area. Her brother Mitch had started out as her partner in the same setup in Duluth, but they divided the business assets when Ash moved to Minneapolis to be with Brianna. One good thing about Minneapolis was the basements. She bought a big house with a huge, underground basement that was easy to outfit and soundproof. The place was located two blocks from Calhoun Square, and until the surgery she'd made a good living. She was amazed at how one surgery and recovery period could practically wipe out one's life savings.

When she was ready to return to work, she called around to put out the word that Tuneworks was up and running again. Right off the bat, The Boys of BabbleOn signed up for studio time, and Hydraulic Woman decided to cut her next disk with Ash. A group that recorded books to tape had hours of work stacked up. Ash felt good that they'd waited for her.

Monday morning, bright and early, the light she had installed instead of a buzzer flashed to let her know someone was at the door upstairs. She opened it to find her friend Stephen looking sheepish and windswept.

"What are you doing here?" she asked as he stepped in. He was a good six inches shorter than Ash with blue eyes, mustache, and crinkles around his eyes. Stephen liked to laugh. She'd known him since junior high school and had always told him if she ever turned into a gay guy, he'd be the one she wanted.

"Can't a guy stop by to visit his good friend every once in a while?"

"I was doing some editing in the studio. Come on down."

She eyed his flannel shirt and painters' pants. "You're decked out in unusual attire for such a clothes horse. What's up?"

"How do you know something's up?"

"You're so transparent, Stephen."

"I'm in scuzzy clothes because I've been working at The Fox." He dropped into the chair at the soundboard. "All right. I admit it. I need you."

"I bet you say that to all the boys."

"Oh, please." He gave her a withering look. "You gotta help us, Ash. This is proving to be a much bigger production than we dreamed of, and we've only got six weeks until it opens."

"Six weeks? Seems like plenty of time."

"You totally don't understand. Please." He rose and paced to one side of the room, then back. "What the hell were we thinking? I saw the play on Broadway. We all saw the movie. Thought the show would be pretty easy. But it's not at all." He brought up the back of his sleeve and gingerly wiped away the invisible perspiration on his forehead. "It's a nightmare. I need your help."

Ash frowned, trying to make her brain function. She imagined her brain looking like that big metal canister at the Gay Days Bingo Parlor, filled with ping pong balls stamped with letters and numbers. She wished she could reach in and pull out a little white ball with the details of Stephen's production on it. No such luck. "Tell me again what you're doing."

He let out a gasp of exasperation. "*Rent*. The musical."

"Oh, yeah. I remember now."

"We're putting the show on as a benefit to save The Fox Theater. The publicist says five performances over Valentine's Day weekend will net the theater at least 60K, enough to pay the back taxes and spruce up the old dame."

"What do you need from me?"

"So much." He sank into the chair again and turned so he was facing her profile. "Sound, baby. I need sound."

"Mics?"

"Way more than that. I've got eight principal cast, seven minor, four understudies, eight musicians, all the instruments, a synthesizer, the PA sound system—it's a nightmare trying to coordinate it all."

"You want to use my studio to practice?"

"No. We're already practicing. The theater works great for that." He cleared his throat.

"Okay, what lame-brained idea is rolling around in that balding skull of yours?"

"Hey! Don't blaspheme my lovely pate." He reached over and tried to fluff her short hair, and she batted his hand away. "Look, I've got two interns from the institute working sound. They're doing the best they can, but the equipment at the theater is not only crappy, there's not enough to go around. And these interns are still learning."

"I see. So you want some more equipment and for me to teach them to get the most out of the theater's soundboard?"

"I want more than that, sweetie. I want you. I want a sound director for this—someone to help me get everything on track and help troubleshoot. Marta, the band director, has her hands full. But you know this music. You know how to attenuate the theater with the gear we have. Hell, you can sing, not to mention follow the score, so you could coach a few of them. You could help me with everything that has to do with the sound. Please." He grabbed her wrist and pulled her to him. "I'll be your bitch. I'll have your baby. I'll come paint your house. I'll clean your house, your studio, your naked body."

She laughed and pushed him back. "Get real, Stephen. Just what I need—a gay houseboy."

"If that's what it takes."

"But Stephen—"

"Don't give me 'but Stephen.' Who was your beard at the high school prom? Who took you to the Boom Boom Room when you

were a young baby dyke? Who introduced you to Silvio & The Sil-
vertones and got you in with the artsy-fartsy musical crowd? Didn't
I vouch for you with all those gay bands and *a capella* groups?"

"Yeah, yeah, I haven't forgotten. I would do almost anything for
you, Stephen, it's just that—" How could she explain that she slogged
through each day as though wading through chest-deep water?

His blue eyes met hers, unwavering. "I know you've had a hard
time, *mi amiga*. I know."

He didn't know the half of it, but he had stood by her these last
months, and she knew she couldn't let him down. "Six weeks?"

"Actually, thirty-nine days."

"Okay."

"You'll do it?"

"Yeah, but you're going to owe me big time." He let out a huge
sigh. "You won't regret it."

The next day, Ash came in the unlocked stage door. Armed with
a clipboard, she passed down a cold hallway lit by one dangling
lightbulb. Clearly the theater had fallen on hard times. Everything
looked grimy and worn. She had never been backstage at The Fox.

She went through an extra-wide doorway into the wings. Dust.
Pulleys. A scattering of dry leaves. Stage techs. Lights strobing on
and off and people hollering directions cross-stage. Everywhere she
looked, people were in motion, some pacing to practice their lines,
others dragging props and backdrops into place. The front of the
house, vacuumed and mopped, always smelled spiffed up for the
audience, but in the wings it was different. The air carried a scent
she'd forgotten, redolent of damp curtains, sweaty old costumes, and
fear. She looked around, wondering where that last scent had come
from. A dark-haired butch in a muscle shirt, jeans, and a very sexy
toolbelt paused in front of Ash and shifted a toothpick on her lip.
"Help you?"

"I'm looking for Stephen Fontaine."

She jabbed her thumb behind her. "Stage left. Talking with the sound techs."

Ash crossed the stage, wondering how the woman stayed warm in such a skimpy top when she herself was shivering in her jacket. Center stage, a man in a baseball cap and black leather jacket and pants spun around as she neared, nearly nailing her with the guitar neck. She instinctively brought her arm to her left breast as she dodged the unplugged red guitar.

"Sorry," he said.

"No problem." Roger. He's Roger, I bet. He looks the part. "Ash, baby, what a sight for sore eyes."

"Obviously, you need glasses."

Stephen introduced her to his two sound techs, Karla and James, both of whom looked young enough to be Ash's children. After Stephen finished listing all the things Tarrant Tuneworks had accomplished, the interns were wide-eyed and looking worried.

"Don't listen to him, you guys. He's making half of that up. I hardly know Jimmy Jam."

Stephen came out from behind the soundboard and put an arm around her shoulders. "Today we're doing a very rough run-through. You can meet the cast and musicians and get an idea of where we are. You also need to meet the band director, the lighting guy, our prop master, the crew. Oh, my." He flipped his thinning hair back dramatically. "So much to do, so little time." He checked his wristwatch. "Good lord, it's time to get started. Grab a chair." He sashayed out into the middle of the stage to call everyone to order.

Ash planted herself on a creaky metal chair stage left and took a pen from her jacket pocket. Her eyes came to rest downstage, below the proscenium arch over the orchestra pit where the band was milling around with their equipment and instruments. Nobody was paying the slightest attention to Stephen. He put two fingers to his lips and let out a shrill whistle, and there was a moment of silence.

"Guys, guys, let's go. I need Mark and Roger center stage. Marta," he called out, "the band ready?" She gave a salute and stepped up on the box above the musicians.

Ash sat quietly and watched the show unfold in fits and starts, fumbles and stops. The voices of the male characters ranged from adequate to terrific. Angel, played by an amazingly tall Latino man with long, wavy dark hair, had a lovely voice with great range, and both Roger and Mark were excellent.

The three main female characters—Joanne, Mimi, Maureen— looked very different from one another. Tall, medium, short. Black, White, and Latina. Angry, tired, and shy.

At first, Ash didn't know who played which part. Then the tall, angry Black woman stepped up into the scene with the men, and Ash realized she was Joanne. She had good stage presence and a nice tone to her voice, but little vocal range.

Soon Ash determined the short, shy Latina was Mimi, and the remaining woman had to be Maureen. Mimi's first scene with Roger was good, but right in the middle of it, Mimi's microphone sputtered and went out.

"Dammit!" Stephen hollered. "James! Karla! Somebody get her another mic."

Angel said, "Say, honey, I don't want to be whiny, but we've got shit for equipment. Mine won't even clip on right."

Karla hollered, "Give us a sec. Let's try the battery first."

While the sound techs scurried around, Ash made a note on her clipboard, then got up to look at the soundboard. She scouted around the console and tracked the electrical cords. Downstage she squatted and looked at the stage speakers. They'd seen better days, though the loudspeakers pointing out to the audience seemed solid. She rose and made some notes on her clipboard. The scar on her chest crawled and tickled. She raised the clipboard, wincing, and hugged it against her. She hoped the unevenness of her chest wasn't noticeable in her baggy shirt.

She didn't even realize she was scowling until the Maureen character was suddenly in her face. Ash flinched and let out a startled squeak.

"Who are you?" The woman's voice was smooth, but somehow dangerous.

"Ash. Ash Tarrant." The woman looked down, nearly to the floor, then swept her gaze up Ash's physique all the way to her eyes.

"I mean, what are you doing here?"

"Sound analysis."

"As opposed to unsound analysis?" Her dark eyes glittered against very pale skin. Smudged half-circles under her eyes stood out in contrast. Her blonde hair formed a very short cap of spun gold, and she wore baggy black sweats and white Reeboks.

Before Ash could answer, Stephen interrupted them. "Maureen, please find your marks."

She turned away, then looked over her shoulder. "I'm Maureen, by the way."

"In the show?"

"In real life." Her voice was low and sultry. "I'm someone else entirely different in the show."

The man playing Roger leaned into his best glam-rock pose and pointed his guitar at Maureen. "Don't let her get to you. She probably changes her name to Maria for *West Side Story* and Dorothy for *The Wizard of Oz.*"

Stephen clapped his hands. "Okay, people, we don't have all night. Let's take it from the top of 'Light My Candle' where Mimi comes in."

Ash hastened out of the way, and the rehearsal went back to its herky-jerky pace. She soon learned the band's pickup amps cut in and out, and the actors' clip-on wireless mics were unreliable. During another mic failure, she jumped down from the stage and wandered over to introduce herself to Marta, the band director, a six-foot-tall Amazon with a multitude of facial piercings. Ash wasn't sure how many. She lost count at fifteen and didn't want to seem rude for staring.

Rather than clamber back up on the stage, Ash moved back six rows and plunked down in a plush seat near the center of the theater. The Fox might be crumbling around them, but the seats were fairly new and much more comfortable than the folding chair stage left.

She watched the crowd onstage. Mark, Roger, Mimi, the homeless characters, Collins, Benny, the cops, the junkies. It was a jumble up there with no one knowing where, exactly, to park themselves. She wondered who the choreographer was. Angel and the Coat Vendor had great rapport. The song neared the end, and all of a sudden, the Maureen character shot out of a row of junkies and bellowed out a question to Joanne. Maureen was no longer clad in black sweats. From neck to ankles, she wore a skintight black leotard that accentuated the ballet-like muscularity of her legs, abs, and shoulders. She was very thin, her smooth movements almost cat-like.

Some of her part was sung, but it was mostly a tour-de-force performance piece. The other actors and the crowd hung back, and after Maureen finished, they moved quickly into the next songs until the act was over.

"Take five," Stephen called out. Most of the cast deserted the stage in relief. He shielded his eyes and looked out into the empty house. "Ash?"

"Yo."

"See what I mean?"

"Oh, yeah. You need so much gear I can't even calculate the cost."

"What can you do with about eight hundred bucks now? I can get more after the show opens."

"Enough to get by, I think. When do you rehearse again?"

"Tomorrow afternoon. And then not again until Friday."

"Okay, I'll see what I can do."

"Don't you want to stay for Act II?"

"No." She tucked the clipboard under one arm, put her cold hands into her jeans pockets, and headed for the stage door. "I've got a lot of work to do, and I'm too tired. I'll be back tomorrow."

Ash pulled her van up to the theater's stage doors as James and his friend, Philip, came strolling up. She got out and said, "Hey, James. Want to give me a hand?"

He unlocked the stage door and came out with a rolling cart. It took them three trips to load up everything, and they worked quickly to lay out the lines, floor monitors, and extra side-fill speakers. Phillip wasn't a sound tech intern, but he was savvy enough to catch on about how to prep the mics. She showed him how to lay them out, ready for the actors.

When Stephen arrived ninety minutes later, Ash was at the soundboard with Karla and James doing speaker and amp checks. Stephen nearly skipped over. "You came back."

She stood up stiffly. "Of course. Why wouldn't I?"

"Oh, I thought we might have scared you away."

"This is one butch who doesn't frighten easy."

"Thank God." He pointed at the mics Phillip was unwrapping. "This is wonderful. I'm going to melt into your arms, girlie."

"No, you're not," she said sternly. "You keep your hands off the merchandise." But then she smiled. "What I want to know is where the hell your stage manager is."

"I haven't been able to get one. Poor, pitiful me. I've got to do it all, baby. I sure could use a stage manager. Know of anybody?"

"Nah. And with my winsome personality, I don't think you want me to be the one out there beating the bush."

"Beating whose bush?" Maureen grinned as she and the tool-belted stage crew worker came strolling past the console. "Maureen," Stephen asked. "How's that tickle in your throat?"

"Fine. It passed."

"I'm so relieved it's not a cold." He turned back to Ash. "You're going to need extra time to get everyone set, aren't you?"

"I'll make it quick."

Two hours into rehearsal, the actors seemed more at ease. New mics, better speakers, and all the adjustments Ash, Karla, and James made had paid off. Only one other major problem arose when Roger's electric guitar went out, but Ash and James laid new lines and quickly restored the connection. Otherwise, by Act II, the mics were operating perfectly, and the actors claimed they could hear themselves much better with the new monitors. Karla and James had the soundboard under control, so Ash went to sit in the auditorium a few rows behind Stephen.

She closed her eyes and listened to Mark and Mimi, Roger and Maureen singing the "Happy New Year" song. She was tired, but she felt a sense of satisfaction at the work she'd done. She could tell a huge difference in the sound, even though the actors were still stumbling all over one another's parts. Stephen stopped them several times and backed them up to go over timing. "Be patient, and you'll all get it. We have a lot of practice ahead of us. Just relax and take your time. Let's move on to Joanne and Maureen's song."

Ash's eyes snapped open. So much of *Rent,* in her opinion, was the boys' show, but in this song, the two women's relationship was finally spotlighted. Joanne strode out from the wings and situated herself on a tall stool. The band began to play the syncopated rhythm of "Take Me or Leave Me." Maureen had quite a long section of the song, and she sounded great. Today she was in a bright orange leotard, and she flitted around Joanne like a flame around a moth, but Joanne sat stiffly, her dreadlocks falling into her eyes, as if she didn't know what to do with herself. Ash shook her head. No, that wouldn't do. They needed to interact more. Joanne came in right on time, but it was as if she couldn't keep up with Maureen. Stephen didn't stop them, but Ash saw the set of his shoulders.

When the number was over, he put an arm across the back of the chair next to him and looked back at her. "Could you work with them, Ash? I'd like to break up into smaller groups now. You can see what's needed, can't you?"

Before she could answer, he stood and pointed toward the Roger and Mimi characters. "Dirk and Sandra, next I'd like to work on 'Without You' here on the stage. Meanwhile, the rest of you, please go downstairs and run through your dance moves with Cedric. And Maureen and Elissa, will you go off with Ash and William to fine-tune 'Take Me or Leave Me'?"

It turned out Maureen's real name *was* Maureen. The Joanne character was Elissa. Ash followed William, the piano player, through a door near the band and introduced herself to him. When they entered the tiny practice room backstage, the two women were glaring at each other. Ash looked longingly at the divan in the corner, but she thought she'd better stay on her feet. William went to the piano and played the opening bars. Maureen launched into her part. Ash tried to ignore the tension, but it soon became apparent the only rapport Elissa and Maureen had was bad.

Ash waved. "Hold it, William." She turned to Maureen. "What seems to be the problem here?"

Maureen shrugged. "I don't have a problem."

"Me neither," Elissa huffed out.

"Is it me?" Ash asked. "I know you two don't really know me, but is that it?"

Maureen laughed.

Elissa glared. "It's not you. But when I volunteered for this part last fall, I didn't sign on to work with her. It was supposed to be Shannon Segal."

Maureen crossed her arms over her chest. "Well, Shannon moved, and I can't help it if I'm not her. I'm not holding the past against you, Elissa."

"I'm holding it against *you*, Maureen."

"Oh—kay," Ash said. "Look, you're both experienced actresses and terrific singers. Can you both please close your eyes and focus on doing the singing thing?"

"I can," Maureen said. Elissa let out a sigh and sank into a folding chair.

Ash nodded. "Let's get the timing down, then we can figure out how to get some of the right kind of electricity."

Elissa took a deep breath and pressed her lips together.

"William," Ash said. "Pick it up four bars from Joanne's entrance."

Maureen sang her lines with aplomb, and Elissa came in with confidence. They faltered a bit but made it to the end.

"Nice. That's great. Now Elissa, try imagining Maureen is someone you actually like—even if you have to look past her ear and pretend to be seeing someone else. Please don't let your frustration show until the end where you're supposed to be getting mad. Use your anger there, but not sooner. Can you try to suppress it early in the song?"

"Hell if I know."

She sounded so petulant Ash wanted to laugh. She took a deep breath instead. "Let's take it from the top and see how it goes." William pounded out the opening notes. Maureen launched into the song and flitted around Joanne, very feline, very sinuous. Ash stopped her twice to work on phrasing and timing, then let them go through it from start to finish. She heard voices out in the hallway and looked at her watch. Twenty minutes had passed, and Stephen had probably called a break. "Time out, people. Thanks, William." She gave him a nod. "Let's take a few moments for a break, then try it with Stephen again."

Elissa flounced out of the room followed by William. When Ash glanced back at Maureen, she'd sunk down on a low divan. Ash paused in the doorway. "You okay?"

Maureen's head came up slowly. "Jesus. That takes a lot of energy."

"Ex?"

"She left *me*, and she's the one who's mad. Does that make any sense?" Maureen rose. "I shouldn't taunt her by pretending there's something between me and Toolbelt Girl, but doesn't a girl get to have a little pride?"

Ash backed into the hallway. "You both sounded a lot better once she relaxed. I think you'll do all right."

"Don't count on it."

While the rest of the cast continued to tighten up their performances, Elissa and Maureen struggled, especially in the scenes where they had to touch each other or kiss. Two weeks later, Stephen blew up. He walked up the center aisle to the edge of the stage and hollered, "What is wrong with the two of you?" He shook a fist in the air. "You each had a fab audition. I've seen both of you excel in other productions. Why can't you get past the personal? Dammit, you're actors!" He ran his hands through his thinning hair. "Helen, you're the understudy. Which part do you want?"

Helen, who looked all of sixteen, blanched. "Neither. I'm Mimi's understudy. I can't do these other parts. Joanne's voice is too deep, and ohmigod I could never sing that cow scene of Maureen's."

Stephen vaulted up onto the stage and rose to full height, pacing like a banty rooster. "Something's got to change."

Elissa held a sheaf of music in her hand. She looked down at it, then tossed it to the floor like an old-fashioned gauntlet. "Obviously nothing's going to change. So that's it. As the song says, I'm gone." Hands on hips, mouth open, Stephen watched as she stomped off.

Maureen's comment, though softly spoken, came through her mic loud and clear. "I guess we know the answer now to her part of the 'Take Me or Leave Me' song."

"Oh, God." Stephen's voice rose. "How am I going to find someone else? We're two flippin' weeks from opening night." Hands still on his hips, he spun a quarter-turn and looked out into the house. "Ash? Ash, can you help me out here?"

"Nuh-uh. No way." Just the thought of being part of the ensemble under the bright lights made her want to toss her cookies. She hadn't had a part in a musical since she was Ado Annie in *Oklahoma* her junior year in high school. Though she sang well enough, it was the last year she could play the femme role musicals seemed to require. The director had been on her back through the *Oklahoma* practices all through that autumn. She was too stocky. She walked too confidently. She wasn't feminine enough. I'm too much of a butch, that's all. Always have been, always will be.

"Ash?" Stephen called out.

She sat slumped in the fifth row, her heart beating like timpani, and she knew Stephen was not going to relent.

"Stand in for today, okay?" he said. "Please? I'll figure something out by next week."

She wasn't sure how she managed to get her feet under her and walk to the stage. Once up there, he rearranged the tall stool so it was exactly center stage and patted it. "Just sit here and let Maureen do all the work. You know the music. You can fake your way through it for Maureen's benefit."

Ash settled against the stool, arms crossed, and one boot heel hooked into a rung. Stephen signaled the band, and the first notes rang out. Ash liked this peppy and playful song. The two characters had quite the skirmish, one wary, the other proceeding with reckless abandon. She was glad her part was the wary one. Maureen had to carry well over half of the song from the beginning until Ash's entrance, so Ash sat back and watched her work.

With a toss of her blonde head, Maureen belted out the first lines. Ash saw dark eyes examine her, then glance away. Was that pain in Maureen's eyes? Fear? Worry? Ash wasn't sure. Her eyes never left the singing, prancing woman. Maureen came close, draped an arm around Ash's shoulder, purred a suggestive line, then whirled away.

Ash watched her, transfixed. A shiver started in the center of her back and rippled through her, leaving goose bumps. Maureen's voice was silky and sexy. Ash's mouth went dry. Maureen slinked back over and pressed up against her, her perfume wafting lightly in the air. Her part was coming to an end, and in Ash's stomach, a hundred butterflies took flight, all fluttering out of formation. The air felt thick and heavy, and Ash had trouble breathing.

Maureen's verse ended. Ash didn't trust her voice, but when she opened her mouth to sing, it came out clear and strong. She focused on the odd syncopation and tried to stay on tempo. As the words she and Maureen sang to one another started to turn into disagreement, then anger, Ash slid off the stool and tried to use her size as if to intimidate, but Maureen was too close in height. She met Ash's gaze, eyes twinkling, and reached out as if to push Ash away. Her hand, though aimed at the middle of Ash's chest, ended up off-center. Ash stepped back with a gasp and stumbled over her line. She couldn't get back on tempo.

"Okay, stop there," Stephen called out. Marta signaled to the band.

Ash, face flaming, looked helplessly toward Stephen. "Sorry." She couldn't say anything else.

Stephen was all smiles. "Ash, baby, you're in particularly good voice today."

Someone let out a low whistle, and someone else muttered, "Now *that's* what I'm talkin' 'bout."

Marta waved her baton. "You ask me, I'd say those two have the right chemistry. Why don't you offer Ash this role permanent-like?"

Ash opened her mouth to protest, but Stephen shouted, "Excellent idea!"

"Wait a minute," Ash finally said. "Shouldn't the Joanne character be Black?"

"Oh, please. This isn't New York. If you haven't noticed, our Angel is Latino, and Collins is definitely not Black."

Miguel, the guy playing the Angel character, let out a snicker and pointed at Collins. "*Mi familia* is scandalized that I've taken up with a White guy. I keep trying to tell them he's more vampire than Anglo-Saxon."

Collins, who was covered in tattoos and in real life rode a Harley, stuck his tongue out at Miguel. He swaggered across the stage, hiking up his leather pants, and said, "You sound good, Ash. I got roped in like you did. Roll with it. Besides, if we really copied the New York production, we'd have to kick out our little blonde Maureen, and then who'd do the dreaded cow scene?"

Ash tucked her hands, which were suddenly like lumps of ice, into the pockets of her jeans. "Stephen, might I have a word with you?"

A warm hand grasped her forearm, and Maureen's brown eyes peered into hers. She was so close Ash could see tiny flecks of gold in the dark brown.

"It's not me, is it?"

"No, no. Of course not. It's just—not really—I'm—"

"Ash," Stephen said, "you can make this role work. You've got the perfect range for all of the songs. Just play yourself. Brassy. Bossy. In control. You know, pretend you're in your own studio."

Maureen let go of her arm and stepped back, leaving Ash feeling chilled. It wasn't the singing that worried Ash, but she knew she could never explain that what really haunted her was how vulnerable she felt, how laid wide open. Her heart beat entirely too close to the surface with nothing at all protecting it. It didn't help that she wasn't sure she could handle all the emotions from the play, not to mention the footlights, the music, the movement. No safety, nowhere to hide. Even the wings, where half the company waited, offered no haven.

Stephen waved his hand. "Earth to Ash. Just think of it as another stage—similar to your studio—and hey, who's better than you in this kind of environment?"

Ash winced. *I'm a techie, not a performer. Why doesn't he know that?*

"How about we take it from the top?" Stephen said. "Let's give it another try,"

She reached one hand behind her for the stool and grabbed hold of its smooth wood like it was a life preserver. Oh, lord, she thought. I have to figure out how to do this. She sat back on the stool as Maureen approached, a lioness in graceful stride.

She sidled up and slid a hip between Ash's knees. Her hand covered her mic, so what she whispered wasn't broadcast. "We can make this work, can't we? Can you sing with me?"

Ash smiled. "I'm a virgin at this, but I'll try." Her mic was live, and her comment came out loud and clear over the PA. She heard muffled laughter, and the sound techs in the wings snickered. Ash turned and gave them a mock evil eye. "I can admit my limitations, James. Now give me a bit more side-fill. I can't hear my own singing over Miss Belt-It-Out here." She smiled at Maureen and was gratified to see the relief flooding the other woman's face.

Now how do I make it through the part late in the play where I have to kiss this woman?

"Listen up, people," Stephen said. "We've only got a few more practices before the dress rehearsal. I think you're doing marvelously on the musical numbers, but we've got to get the transitions down. Today all we're going to do is work on that one thing. Transitions. Full lighting today, too. Let's get all the parts synchronized. Okay, take it from the top with Mark's narration."

Ash stood with other cast members and watched the opening sequence. After a while, she retreated into her own thoughts. Her scar ached. All day long she'd felt like her left breast was still there, even though she knew it wasn't. She'd heard of phantom limbs before, but phantom tits? The image made her laugh, and she was still smiling when Maureen came up on her right side and tucked her arm into Ash's. Ash had grown accustomed to letting Maureen into her personal space.

Over the music, Maureen said, "How're we doing?"

"Not bad. You're late."

"Traffic." She squeezed Ash's arm. "Want to go out for cappuccino afterwards?"

"Cappuccino?"

"Yeah. To celebrate. I finally got a job."

"No kidding. That's great. I don't really drink cappuccino, though."

"They've got chai and other teas at the place I'm thinking of. Anything non-alcoholic would work for me."

"You don't drink?"

"Not at the moment." The band struck up the familiar chords of the song "Rent," and Maureen said, "Uh-oh. We're up in a minute." She gave Ash's arm another squeeze and let go. "Better get my ass in gear." She tore off, hustling toward the darkened stage.

The rehearsal went very well. Ash felt like her head spun at times, especially during the song "Tango: Maureen," which was a duet with Mark. She and the actor managed very well together despite her towering over him by five inches.

The only part Ash worried about came toward the end of Act II when she and Collins and the company sang "I'll Cover You." The group of friends was falling apart then, and it was a breakup of sad proportions. Her part wasn't tough to sing, but it pulled all of her emotions out of their hiding places.

She hadn't seen the original play on the stage, and though she'd listened to the soundtrack often enough over the years, being part of a live show was a lot different. Roger and Mimi's ill-fated lives, Angel's death, the breakup of friends and lovers . . . all of it was so evocative. And the implosion of the Joanne and Maureen characters' relationship sent ripples of recognition through her. Brianna had failed to "cover" her, and every time she heard the song, it brought it all back. Oh, shit. I hope I don't break down over that. I can't stand how sad this is. And yet there was also such energy. She felt as though she were taking part in a sacred rite. She had only glimpsed that bonding in high school and college productions from the wings, a spectator to the real action. Now each time the company staggered into the rousing finale, she heard the play's musical slogan, "No Day But Today," and the words echoed in her head for hours.

She thought about the fact that, like the song said, there really truly were only five hundred twenty-five thousand six hundred minutes in a year, and how was she measuring those minutes? How had she been living them? Half of that amount, over the last six months, had been spent in a dark funk so low, so lifeless, and so anguished she hardly understood how she'd survived it.

Before that? She didn't think she'd experienced half the joy in her whole life that she was feeling as this production came together.

Rehearsal didn't end until nine p.m., and Ash felt drained, but she couldn't turn down Maureen's plea to go out for cappuccino— and some food.

"Follow me in your van," Maureen said. "I'm parked around the corner in the dark green beater."

Maureen led Ash about a mile to a place off Lyndale where she pulled her old Chrysler in front of a café lit up with red, green, blue, and orange Christmas lights around all the windows. It hadn't snowed for two days, and the sidewalk was clear, but there was a chilly bite in the air.

Maureen joined her in front of Shooting Star's Grill & Café. "This is the place," she said.

"Love the lights."

"She leaves them up year-round. Makes the place seem quaint. Wait'll you see the inside."

Ash passed through the door into a shadowy room. A twenty-foot-long Oriental carpet in deep rich maroon and blue hues led to the cashier. The booths were tall and red, nine little oases of privacy, four on one side, five on the other. All the light in the seating area came from a series of tiny golden bulbs in funky-looking wall sconces about six feet apart around the room. In between, cloth twisted into silver and gold chains and swatches of multi-colored scarves adorned the walls. The swirls and splashes gave the impression of movement and color and coziness.

As they walked to the counter, Ash looked up and realized all that was missing were Chinese lanterns. Without a doubt, this place had once been a Chinese restaurant. But now it was a simple café with soups, sandwiches, coffee, and tea.

On closer inspection, the man behind the counter was a woman. Ash looked up at six and half feet of long, lean, caftan-clad femininity topped with carrot-colored red hair. Her eyes were heavily made up, but the warmth was unmistakable.

"Star," Maureen said, "this is my friend Ash, also known as Joanne."

Star smiled and reached an enormous hand across the counter. "Ah, so this is the one. Well, honey, I'll be there for all the performances, and I'm simply insisting on crashing the dress rehearsal. I love the theater. I love Rent. I simply adore Angel. I love it all." She let go of Ash and said, "How are you enjoying rehearsals? I hear you got sucked in unexpectedly."

"Very true. Maybe you ought to be the one in the role."

"Oh, honey, if you ever need a six-foot-plus MTF who can't sing worth beans, call me up. Somehow I don't think I would do for this role at all." She grinned, and Ash couldn't help smiling back. "So what are you girls up for tonight? A little chicken cheddar or beef barley soup? Perhaps a croissant sandwich?"

"Definitely soup," Maureen said. "I'm starving." She leaned in close to Ash. "Care to split a sandwich?"

"Sure."

"What kind of soup?"

Ash looked at the menu board. "Chicken cheddar." She reached for the wallet in her back pocket.

"No, no, no," Maureen said. "I'm paying. Put your wallet away. I'm celebrating."

Star's eyes opened wide. "Baby, don't tell me! You got the job?" Before Maureen could even answer, Star was hustling around the counter to wrap her in a bear hug. She lifted her off the ground, twirling, and made her squeal.

"Set me down, Star. Down, girl, down!"

"I'm just so happy for you, sweetheart. So happy."

"Yeah, now maybe I'll be able to pay you the rent."

Star slipped back around the counter and took their orders. "Lucky you came in when you did. I've got just enough soup left. Here's your mugs and tea water, and I'll bring out the rest in a jiffy."

They got situated in a booth, and a wave of fatigue washed over Ash. She let out a sigh and sat back, closing her eyes and willing herself to draw in energy from somewhere, anywhere. Maureen's warm hand squeezed her forearm.

"You look tired, Ash."

"I'm still not quite up to par. I had some—" she paused, but then pressed on "—surgery a few months ago, and I still don't have all my energy back."

"I understand."

Ash leaned forward and put her elbows on the table. "Tell me about the new job."

"It's working in a private high school theater department on the plays they're putting on this year, including a summer school production of West Side Story. It's almost full time for a month or so during each quarter. Sort of all averages out to half time, and it pays well."

"So you'll direct or stage manage or what?"

"Vocal coach." Maureen grinned, her teeth flashing white in the low light. "High school kids can be like herding cats, but then again, sometimes you run into some real talent with these teenagers. And there's already a choreographer and musical director. I can focus on the singing and overall coordination of the music."

"Sounds like a lot of fun."

"I think so, and it will let me try out for more roles around the Twin Cities."

"You're very good, Maureen. You know that, right?"

Maureen ran her hands through her short blonde hair as she blushed furiously. "I love the Maureen role. I think this is a wonderful play. It's a lot of fun, and it's been even better ever since you showed up."

"That's nice of you to say."

Star brought their soup and fussed with silverware and napkins and ice water, then said, "I'll let you girls plot and plan. Just call out if you need anything." She whisked off, her caftan billowing slightly. Ash noticed she wore shoes with only a modest heel, so Star was indeed very tall.

Ash looked back across the table as Maureen asked, "What do you think of Star?"

"She seems nice," Ash said. "You two been friends for long?"

"Over twenty years. Went to high school together. For a time in our late teens and early twenties, Star and I were married. Back then, she was better known as Stan and worked as a window dresser for Dayton's."

"How old are you?"

"Thirty-eight. We divorced when I was twenty-two, but I'll always love starry, starry Stan. He was always my best friend, and now *she's* my best friend. What's your opinion of that?"

"Is Star a good person?"

"The very best."

"Then I adhere to the 'any love is good love' philosophy, and that's enough for me. Are you still together?"

"Oh, no. Not for years and years. I was single for a long time, then with Elissa for three years. She left me before summer started."

"I thought you said something about rent. You must have meant the play?"

Maureen laughed. "No, I live upstairs. In the little apartment above the café. Star lives with her lover in a very big, very swanky place over in Kenwood. I keep an eye on this place and pay her rent."

"Ah, I see."

The food and company gradually revived Ash, and the next hour passed in a flash. She and Maureen talked about their work, favorite plays, foods they liked, music they adored.

Maureen sipped the last of her tea. "When I get a little money, I buy CDs, and if any is left, I buy food and clothes."

Ash laughed. "I thought Erasmus said that about books."

"We all have our vices now, don't we? And music is definitely mine. That, and getting involved with women who can't commit."

"Let's not go there," Ash said, suddenly tired. She checked her watch. "In fact, I think I better get going. I've got an eight a.m. gig."

Maureen walked her to the door and gave her a hug. "Drive carefully. I'll see you tomorrow."

Ash went out to her van and started it up. She sat shivering for a minute, waiting for the engine to warm. When she put it in gear, she thought once more about Brianna. She hadn't ever really committed. What would it be like to be lovers with someone who did? Someone who could be like Angel in the play—or Collins? Somebody who gave her all? She'd had one other long-term relationship, right out of college, and it had only lasted three years. She wondered if there was something wrong with her that she wasn't able to see.

She thought about it all the way home. As she parked the van in her garage, Ash came to the conclusion she wanted a life with someone who loved so much, so strongly, so completely that even if Ash were to die of breast cancer, her lover would stay at her side, praying to have every single minute to revel in right up until the very end. And I want to feel the same way for her—if I can ever find someone like that.

Ash stood in the wings, Maureen on one side, Miguel on the other, waiting with the company for the curtain to go up. The dress rehearsal the day before had been a whirlwind. Star had raved for an hour. They'd only had about sixty people in the house then, so it hadn't seemed quite so nerve-wracking. But now, with a packed house of eighteen hundred, every nerve in her body was wracked.

Stephen made a clucking noise, and the actors parted to allow him to stride up near the curtain in front of them. "It's a marvelous house," he said quietly but with feeling. "Simply unbelievable. The energy. The excitement. Do me proud, all of you. Make the hard work pay off." He gazed around. "You ready, guys?" The actors playing Mark, Roger, and Collins nodded. "Then let's do it."

Ash was so glad she didn't have to be on stage when the curtain went up, but still, her entry into the play came soon enough, and she was sick to her stomach with the anticipation of it. She hardly heard the intro over the pounding in her head, and then the music started. Someone took her hand, someone with a cold, shaking grasp. She looked at Miguel, gave him a false smile, and squeezed his hand.

"Break a leg, honey," he whispered.

"You, too."

Soon enough, she was on—focusing, listening, flowing with the music. They got through "Rent," and then she was off the stage and Maureen was hugging her. "You did good. It's great. It's just—alive!"

Laughter bubbled up, and Ash stood grinning. Alive. Yes, entirely alive.

The rest of the play passed so quickly that later Ash couldn't recall anything but certain flashes of it, but the key pieces she did remember were seared on her retina permanently for later viewing. When she kissed Maureen for the first time, the audience erupted in cheers, followed by amused catcalls. When Angel and Collins sang the first rendition of "I'll Cover You" early on, the energy and excitement was palpable. "La Vie Boheme" was an electric perform-ance, and she didn't even feel awkward with her few dance steps. And then, with the death scene, Ash didn't have to be onstage to know what was happening. The entire theater was awash in tears.

By the time the company sang the "Finale," the audience was on their feet, and for the first time in her life, Ash knew the meaning of "bringing down the house." She'd never experienced anything like it. When they stood before the audience, taking the final bows, it washed over her like waves of warm water, and she floated in it. Stephen came on stage, and the cast bowed to him. Many of them were crying.

When the curtain finally came down, every single one of them, along with every tech, every hand, every understudy, every actor was swept through the doors and into the hallway where they massed in communal hugs, laughing, crying, talking nonsense, and so full of joy that Ash was suddenly thrilled to remember they would get to do this four more times. *How could I ever have been so afraid?* She laughed out loud, knowing that the next night, she'd be just as terrified.

Stephen called out, "Go change so you can meet your adoring public. We've still got schmoozing to do."

Soft arms wrapped around Ash from behind. She turned and found Maureen, her face flushed and eyes shining with pleasure. "Come with me, Ash."

Maureen pulled her along, back toward stage right and through the doorway into a quiet corner near the electrical wiring. "Wow," Maureen said. "What an experience."

"The understatement of my life. My brother was even crying out there."

Maureen moved in closer. They'd already shared so many kisses on stage. They hadn't been an act for Ash, but she knew they probably had been for Maureen. Still she brought her face close to Maureen's and leaned in to press a soft kiss on her lips. Maureen brought her hands up, palms facing Ash, and rested them on the front of Ash's shoulders.

Ash broke off the kiss and stepped back, flushing with embarrassment. She looked down at the front of her, and all of a sudden, the facts of her situation crashed in on her. She realized she'd been playing with fire for days now.

"What's the matter?" Maureen asked. Her eyes sparkled, and she looked so damn beautiful that Ash could hardly breathe. But this could go no further. It would hurt too much. "I can't."

"Oh, yes, you can." Maureen's eyes narrowed, and she slinked forward, very much like her character in the play, all grace and feline sensuality.

Ash stepped back a step, then another. Maureen kept pace until Ash bumped into the wall beside the electrician's table. The cat had her cornered. "Maybe this isn't a good idea."

"Why?" Maureen stood very close, but not touching her. "I'm going through some stuff. I—well, I'm just not—you know."

Maureen pulled up her own shirt, tucked her hands under it, and squirmed. Ash heard a snap, and Maureen pulled out a rounded bundle of material and let it drop to the floor. Ash didn't get a chance to look at it closely before Maureen leaned into her and snuggled up close. "Hold me, Ash."

Nowhere to run, nowhere to hide as Maureen pressed against her. With her heart beating so hard she thought it would come out of her chest, Ash lifted up her arms and wrapped them around Maureen, who tucked her head in next to Ash's neck.

"See how nicely we fit together?" Maureen mumbled into her ear.

Ash could only nod.

Maureen stepped back. She met Ash's eyes and took hold of Ash's right hand. She lifted it up, toward her own chest, pulling the flat of Ash's palm against her shirt. Maureen pressed it firmly against her breast—which wasn't there. Ash pulled her hand back as though she'd been burned.

Maureen said, "They took my left one and yours as well. So we fit together like it was planned that way."

"What?"

"I'm surprised you never noticed. It's not like that prosthetic thing was ever a good match."

"What?"

"Stop saying 'what.' I had breast cancer, Ash. I had surgery two months before you did."

"Wha—how did you know—"

"Stephen told me. I think he was worried that during rehearsal I was going to rake my claws across your chest or hit you, and I'd hurt you, so he'd lose you for the Joanne part."

Ash sagged back against the wall, glad for the solid cement at her back. "Did she—Elissa—leave you because of the—the cancer?"

Maureen shrugged. "It was the final straw. I'd cleaned up my act for the two months before I had the surgery. I stopped drinking and clubbing and smoking cigs. She stood by me through the surgery, but it was over—we were over, I mean. She's still pissed, though, that things ended that way. Feels guilty."

Ash didn't think Brianna felt even the slightest bit guilty. Obviously, Elissa had more character. "I see." She didn't know what to say next.

Maureen tipped her head to the side a little and studied Ash. She reached up and tucked a lock of hair behind Ash's ear. "I know the stage is an unreal place. After all this time, I feel like we're all part of a strange family. And I've been your girlfriend—in the play I mean—now for a couple weeks. I know the situation is artificial. But, Ash, what I feel isn't artificial or temporary. It's real—like how I feel about the guys playing Mark and Roger and Angel and Collins, even though they're real people all mixed up in characters who aren't real. It's hard to explain. All I know is what I feel for you is real."

"Not just because of my—my mastectomy?"

"No."

Ash's next words came out with effort, and she couldn't look at Maureen. "I could see how you might feel a connection to me because I understand about you and your—you know—your own situation."

"No," Maureen said, shaking her head, then holding back a grin. "No. I fell a little in love with you the first time you kissed me on stage. And I knew it for sure that night we went to the café. That first kiss on stage—well, Ash, let's just say I never had to act after that."

Ash's head was clearing, though she was still a little breathless. "I didn't know—didn't even understand my feelings for you when Stephen dragged me onstage, and you sang 'Take Me or Leave Me.' But you woke me up. It was a real shock. I'd felt mostly dead until then, and all of a sudden—whew! You made me feel."

Maureen smiled, and her whole face lit up. "I love singing with you. When we're onstage, you look at me with so much emotion on your face."

Ash swallowed and gazed down at her feet. When she spoke, her voice came out low and quiet. "I look at you like that because I think you're beautiful."

She glanced up and saw Maureen blush, and she knew Maureen would try to change the subject.

"Hey, we're putting on *Wicked* next year—an all-lesbian version. How about I do the Glinda role, and you can be the Elphaba, the Green Girl?"

"Forget that. You should be the Green Girl. You've got tons more acting experience than me. Besides, you've got the range for it, and I don't. Nobody could sing the Green Girl like you could. I'd rather be Fiyero."

"Fiyero? Hmmm, well, he's got a couple of good parts." Maureen stepped closer. "But Glinda and Elphaba sing together so much more."

Ash reached out and took Maureen's hand. "But if I remember correctly, in the end, it's Fiyero who gets the Green Girl." She held her breath as she looked into serious dark eyes.

Maureen leaned in, as if to kiss her. Her lips detoured to the side of Ash's face, and her breath was warm against her ear. "Ash, you've already got the Green Girl."

A jolt of electricity rippled through Ash's body. "Hurray for Fiyero," she whispered, then laughed. She brought her hands up to either side of Maureen's face. "Can I kiss you—for real now?"

"Yes. Please. Any time you want." Ash paused and took a deep breath.

"What is it?" Maureen looked at her, concern in her eyes.

"Do you believe in soul mates?"

Maureen almost seemed to deflate. "Please don't tell me you don't."

"I do now."

"Oh, good." Maureen pressed closer and wrapped her arms around Ash's waist. "We fit together too perfectly for you not to. I *totally* believe in soul mates. And breast friends, too."

PAIGE

Paige Brandt came home on a Friday evening in the spring of 1988 after nine years in the joint upstate. I'd been up to the Skywater High School gym to work out and had stopped to gas up my VW. Parked at the pump closest to the highway at Johnson's Shell Station gave me a good view as the Greyhound rolled into town, stopped at the corner, and she got out. Her light brown, shoulder-length hair blew in the wind. She wore jeans and a sweatshirt, and even from a distance, I saw her shiver in the cool Pacific Ocean air. She held a paper bag in her hand—that was all. A thick, brown grocery-type bag with the top rolled over and the whole thing creased as though she'd held it in her lap for hours, which she probably had. It's nearly two hundred miles from Central Oregon Correctional Facility to this little town of Skywater along the Oregon coast, population 932.

Paige robbed the liquor store seven years ago with Charley Yecke. The Sheriff caught them before they even made it over the Washington border, which was probably lucky in some ways. No federal charges. I heard both of them were high and drunk and completely out of it, sitting on the side of Hwy 101 near Seaside. They didn't put up a fight when they were arrested, and Paige didn't have a chance when it came to trial before Judge Tremont. Though she was only sixteen at the time, they tried her as an adult over the protests of her mother and the legal aid attorney. In a twenty-minute open-and-shut case, her fate was sealed.

The world kept turning while she did her time. I graduated from our shit-hole high school, a place that never gave wild girls a chance. And Paige was definitely a wild one. By fourteen, she'd been drinking and smoking and running with boys four or five years older. Her mama worked at the candy store, pulling taffy, making divinity, cooking up chocolate for fudge and truffles. Nobody knew who Paige's daddy was, and her mama had never married.

Sometimes I thought of her: wild-haired Paige Brandt who stole $760.48 from Pitney's Liquor & Spirits and spent less than a hundred of it before she and Charley were captured. Didn't seem like it was worth it.

News rippled through town that Paige was back. All day Saturday I heard plenty of conversations over the counter at Sweet Lands where I work.

Paige couldn't go "home" anymore. Her mama had died the year before. Ovarian cancer. Paige's granddad let her have a room. Mrs. LaBounty was scandalized to have to live across the street from them. Mister Steele said he'd bought a new box of shotgun shells, just in case.

I work at the candy store as I have since senior year in high school. Paige's mother taught me well. I still miss her.

Monday morning, with the morning sun shining bright, I stood at the window of Sweet Lands Candy Store assembling the ingredients for five colors of frosting. Three trays of cupcakes had come out of the oven an hour ago, and I was fixing to frost and decorate them with little crosses and Jesus faces. Dixie Shenk was due to pick them up right after nine a.m. for the kids in her daughter's class at Holy Redeemer.

If you work long enough at a candy store, eventually sweets no longer hold your interest. I've long since stopped caring about jellybeans and peanut clusters, all-day suckers and saltwater taffy. Tourists come and tourists go, and they can take the damn candy with them. I'm pretty well sick of it.

Paige tapped on the window at 8:55, five minutes before we open, and a thrill of worry sped up my spine. Even though I had wanted to be—had intended to be—less judgmental than the rest of the townspeople, I couldn't help it. She caught me by surprise, before I had the chance to properly compose myself. I met her eyes, and I know she saw the momentary fear. Her face closed off and took on a hardened scowl.

She was dressed exactly the same as the day before, but not holding anything at all, not a gun, not the paper bag, only herself. She crossed her arms over her chest and started to turn away, but I shook my head and mouthed, "Wait."

I had sticky crap all over my hands, so I gave them a quick rinse in the metal sink, then wiped them on my pink apron as I went around the counter. Mister Tilden didn't need to know I opened up early. He was off to Portland to buy another truckload of sugar and oil and what-not. I flipped the Open sign and unlocked the door. She shuffled in, bringing the smell of salt air with her. The fifty years of pain in her eyes looked bad on her twenty-five-year-old face, and her dark eyes didn't burn with the intensity they had in high school. Instead, she reeked of fatigue. Her hair looked like it had been hacked with pinking shears. I was surprised at how pale she was, her high cheekbones not even carrying a hint of color. "You been down to the beach?" I asked.

"Too cold."

I imagined it would be since she wasn't wearing a jacket. The sweatshirt was dark blue and not particularly thick. She must have been wearing it for a long time for it to appear so worn.

She stood in the store, her eyes taking in the shelves of candies, little kid toys, gum, and racks of fancy candy behind glass. I couldn't remember when Mister Tilden had cleared out the tables in the alcove and replaced them with two rows of red shelves, but I knew Paige couldn't have ever seen the change. She turned her back to me, moved over into that alcove, and ran a hand over a display of glittery Barbie candy packs. I suddenly realized she wasn't here to buy any-thing, but to take in the place, as though she were breathing it in.

I didn't know what to say, so I went back around the counter, to the worktable by the window, and resumed frosting the cupcakes. Every once in a while, I glanced over, but Paige seemed lost in thought.

Outside, foot traffic increased in front of my friend Robin's bakery across the street, and I wished for a nice, steamy cappuccino. A big RV hauling a fishing boat pulled up in front and blocked my view. Three teenaged kids spilled out of the back along with three adults from the front. They dodged across the highway to the bakery. I didn't notice Dixie, and she startled me when she came in.

"Good morning, Dixie. And good timing, too. I'm ready to wrap these up for you." I sealed up one box of cupcakes.

Dixie glanced over at Paige, then frowned and moved up close to the counter. In a voice not low enough for Paige to fail to hear, she said, "What's she doing in here?"

I shrugged and turned away, my hands fumbling with the flaps for the second box. I got it together and quickly filled it with the remaining cupcakes, then stacked and carried them over to the counter. "Anything else you need?"

Dixie pressed her lips together and shook her head.

I took her money and rang up the order.

She slid the boxes off the counter and headed for the door in a hurry. "Keep the change, Jillian."

I stood holding the two quarters as Paige turned and sauntered toward the door. She saw Dixie and said, "Here, I'll get that for you," and reached for the door handle.

"No," Dixie said sharply. "I can get it myself."

But by then Paige was pulling the door open and stepping back. Dixie shot her a look of pure malice as she raced out, nearly running into one of the kids munching on a donut near the RV.

So that's how it's going to be, I thought. I didn't know what to say, and when Paige met my eyes, I looked away.

"You went to Skywater High, didn't you?"

I nodded. "Graduated in 1980."

"You were a year behind me." Paige gazed over my head at the Coca-Cola clock. "Have you worked here long?"

"Since my senior year."

Her gaze dropped abruptly, and the eyes that met mine were filled with such longing I very nearly felt my soul sucked right out. "You knew her." It wasn't a question but a statement of wonder. "Oh! You must be Jill. She wrote about you sometimes."

I felt my face grow hot. Paige's mother sent letters to the prison with my name in them? How strange. I didn't know what to say.

"You're not hiring here, are you?"

"Sorry. We're full up at the moment. But lots of places will be needing summer help soon."

She turned away. "All right then, thanks."

"You're welcome, Paige."

For a moment she looked startled that I called her by her name. She trudged toward the door, and I watched her go. I didn't think she'd have an easy time finding work.

Days passed, and talk didn't let up about "that vicious felon" and "Aggie Brandt's sleazy daughter." In the Coffee Café, I got an earful from four older guys who sat behind me. Almost made me too sick to eat my omelet. The checkers at Fenton Foods carried on a continual conversation with one another about Paige as they rang up my groceries. In the laundromat, a woman with three pre-school-aged kids running around raising hell complained that she didn't feel her children were safe in Skywater anymore. Obviously, Paige's arrival was the biggest thing to happen in town since the Weed & Feed store got held up last fall.

One day I drove up to Florence, thirty miles up the coast, and Paige Brandt was a topic of discussion at the Dairy Queen where I stopped for a cone.

Only my mother seemed to have any perspective. "People change in nine years, Jillian. That girl went into jail a cocky but scared sixteen-year-old kid, and now, after all this time, she's probably a different person. People shouldn't judge her until they get to know who she is now."

I agreed with my mother, but the two times I had seen Paige in town, she'd stalked by me, her face angry and hard—like she wanted to kill somebody. Really, the townspeople here are merciless. I don't know how she stayed. I'm not even sure why I had.

A couple of weeks went by, and talk around town died down, then turned to the Turnbull girl's pregnancy and whether senior baseball shortstop Jack Clark was the father or not. I heard so many heated discussions on the topic that soon I was sick to death of it, but here was Mister Kaiser, standing at my counter asking for truffles while yammering on about malicious girls who deep-six the sports careers of well-meaning athletes. Give me a break. As much as we needed the business at Sweet Land, I wish the townsfolk would buy their candy then go somewhere else to gossip. Thank God it was closing time.

As Mister Kaiser was leaving, Paige came through the door. She wore a navy-blue windbreaker and jeans. I looked at the clock and saw it was two minutes to eight, then turned to finish wiping down the fudge table.

I got that funny feeling you get when someone is staring—sort of a shiver of apprehension. When I looked up, I saw Paige looking at me from the alcove by the miniature Superman lunchboxes. She turned away, but not before I saw her look of embarrassment

I asked, "Can I help you with anything in particular?"

She glanced up, blushing. Her face was hard to read, but she looked reflective, like she had something to say but couldn't quite come out with it.

Just then, Mister Tilden came up from the back room. "Jillian, I've got one last receipt. Have you cashed out the—hey!" He glared toward Paige. "What are you doing in here?"

Paige's face went slack, her eyes hard and narrowed. Before she had a chance to answer, Mister Tilden was at the door, pulling it open. "You can take your thieving self right out the door, and don't come back."

I raised a hand and said, "Mister T—"

"Hush now." He nodded toward the clock. "It's after hours. Who knows what she has in mind. C'mon, Brandt, get out."

Paige took a deep breath and moved slowly toward the door. Her hands were balled into fists, and she shook with fury. She stopped at the doorway. "I didn't want your crass shit anyway."

He grabbed her arm and forcefully pushed her out. "I catch you back here, your ass is grass." He slammed the door shut, turned the lock, and pulled down the Closed shade.

Out the main window, I caught sight of Paige standing on the sidewalk to light a cigarette. She looked toward me as though she wanted to tell me something, but I was hard-pressed to know what it could be. Her head went up, and she squared her shoulders before she hurried away.

Exasperated, Mister Tilden put his hands on his hips and faced me. "I don't understand how Aggie could have been such a wonderful person, and her daughter is the opposite. How is that so?"

I didn't know how to answer, but I don't think Mister T would have cared what I said.

"If that tramp shows up here again, Jillian, you are to call 9-1-1. You hear me?" I nodded, and he said, "Okay, finish up here, and I'll see you in the morning."

My boss retreated to the rear of the store and left me with the last of the day's pans to wash. As I stood over the sink, I saw a flash of red outside. Paige stood at the window looking down at the trays of goodies I had so artfully displayed there. When her eyes rose to meet mine, they were full of such sadness and longing that I had to look away.

Working all day in the candy store is hard on me. I'm shy, and the steady flow of customers and their demands makes me feel like they're sucking all the sweetness right out of me. Whenever I get the early shift, I like to jog or walk along the beach in the late afternoon. Great stress relief, even when the weather is bad, and I get some time to myself. I take a change of clothes to work for those early mornings, and most days, when I get done at 2:30, I try to get at least half an hour of exercise, then go home and wash away the salt from the ocean and the sugar from the shop.

Once the high school lets out for the summer, the gym is open to the public three days a week. I often go up there to shoot a few baskets, lift weights, and don gloves to smack the punching bag. On a rainy day like today, though, I usually stay indoors.

I drove my VW up to the school. Built in the Fifties, it's a rabbit warren full of dark hallways and shabby rooms. I don't think they've painted since I graduated. It smells of dampness, dust, and floor cleaner. Mel and Jorge, the custodians, had cordoned off the gym to re-seal the wood floor, so I took the stairs to the upper loft where the Universal Gym sat surrounded by benches and free weights. The windowless room had never had proper ventilation, and it was much warmer than the sixty-degrees outside. All was quiet and no one else was working out.

Feeling energized by the prospect of solitude, I stepped across mats to the far wall, set down my little workout bag, then sank to the floor to stretch. I had changed back at the store into shorts, a T-shirt, and a black Mickey Mouse sweatshirt. I shifted into a hurdler's stretch, then a variety of other contortions to loosen up. My legs were fatigued from standing most of the day, but my arms felt strong. I decided to focus most on upper body lifting.

I started to rise and heard a distant rhythmic pounding. Bump-bump-bump . . . pause. Bump-bump-bump . . . Through the door and down the hall was a room, hardly more than a twelve-by-twelve-foot box, where two huge boxing bags hung in the corners. I opened the door and ducked into the dim room before I realized it was Paige Brandt pounding the hell out of the big black bag. She wore red shorts, a baggy gray T-shirt, and brown gloves on her hands. When she turned toward me, her face glowed so red she looked like she'd been crying. I hesitated. She whirled away and slammed a fist into the bag. Huffing with exertion, she struck at it again.

I watched, fascinated, until she paused and stared at me. "What are you looking at, candy girl?"

I glanced away, heart in my throat. She resumed her assault on the bag, so I went to the corner and rooted around in the box full of gloves until I found a pair to fit. The gloves were bulky and a little unwieldy, but the rules, posted prominently on the wall, required that no one work the bags without gloves. The insides were stiff and rough against my palms, and I flexed my hands to try to loosen them.

I went to the left bag and gave it a half-hearted poke. Paige peppered her bag with jab after jab, then leaned in, steadied the swinging bag with her left fist, and bashed away with her right glove. I let fly a volley of punches, but I couldn't stop watching her out of the corner of my eye. I wondered if they let women box in prison. I wondered if she'd had to defend herself there. Suddenly, I wondered if I was safe in the same room with her.

As if to answer my question, she squared off and faced me, fists curled up against her chest. "What is wrong with you—with all you people?"

Now that I looked closer, I saw she had indeed been crying. Her chest heaved, perhaps less from the exertion with the punching bag and more from emotions I easily read in her face. "I can't speak for the rest of the town."

She stepped nearer. "I shouldn't have come here."

"What?" I didn't understand. Did she mean she shouldn't have come to the gym? Or to Skywater? I let my hands drop to my sides as I studied her. She brought one glove up to her forehead as though to brush bangs out of her face, but the glove was too bulky.

"Paige." I moved forward, mouth open, but not knowing what to say.

"You think you're better than me." A glove reached out, tapped me on the shoulder, bumping me back. When the next jab came toward me, I blocked it with my right arm. "Not one person gives a shit what I've been through."

I blocked another jab and met her eyes. "You want to beat someone up, Paige?" She didn't respond. "Go on—hit me. Just stay away from my face."

She lashed out, a roundhouse that whacked me hard on the left shoulder. Holding my gloves high, I braced myself for another hit. Instead, I saw misery well up and leak out of her eyes. She turned her face away, defeated.

An unexpected rush of heat started at my throat and traveled straight to my groin. I reached out and touched her chest with the top of my glove. I moved closer, pushed her with the glove again. She stepped aside, alarm showing on her tear-stained face, and I followed as she backed toward the closed door. "You want to hurt someone, Paige?" She shook her head. "I gotta go."

Once again, I met her eyes, and before she looked away, I felt fire rise up in my belly. For a moment I couldn't breathe. I tightened my fist in the glove and socked her in the shoulder. "Come on, Paige. You're a chicken."

Now her eyes blazed, and she brought up her fists. I shoved her back against the door. "Jillian, I could hurt you badly. Don't provoke me."

I grinned and cuffed her again, a light blow to her other shoulder. She struck out and caught me by surprise. I didn't have time to react as a brown glove sank into my mid-section and ejected all the air from my body. I let out a gasp and would have fallen to the ground had she not grabbed me. "I'm sorry . . . so sorry. God, I'm sorry! How many times do I have to say it?"

We stumbled, clutched together like two prizefighters in a clinch, but there was no referee to part us. When I got my breath back, it exploded from me in a blaze of panting. My whole body was electrified, every nerve ending quivering. I wrapped my arms around her middle and squeezed, pressed my face into her neck, sucked on salty skin. She stiffened, as though surprised.

"Paige," I whispered as I pressed her against the door, moved my knee between her legs, and heard her moan.

Her arms tightened around me, the gloves against my shoulders. She was leaning so hard against my gloves they were pinned against the door behind her. I was able to slide my hands out. I reached up under her T-shirt, caressed her ribs, kneaded firm moist breasts, and pressed my ear against her neck. The pulse point there raced as fast as my breathing.

She moved against my leg and made a whimpering sound, like a wounded animal. I froze and leaned back slowly, afraid of what I would see in her eyes.

Her irises were huge, a well of deep brown pain. "You smell like she used to, Jill. Just like cotton candy." The brown gloves came up on either side of my head and pulled my face toward her. Soft lips covered mine, drank me in, devoured me. Somehow she got her boxing gloves off, and her hands went up my shirt and unhooked my bra. Hot palms glided around to cover my breasts, and I gripped her waist, my thumbs digging into her hip bones.

She shifted her hips forward, moved her knee, and suddenly I was impaled upon her leg, the center of me rubbing against her with abandon. She cupped my behind, moved me up higher, and I pulled up my shirt. Her mouth found my right breast and sent shock waves to the hot bundle of nerves between my legs.

It was all I could do to hold on then. I was a throbbing, pulsing being, feeling a high I had never before experienced, eagerly tasting her tongue, her mouth, her neck. My hand found its way into her shorts, down into the patch of soft hair, to the moist wetness within. She gasped and gripped me tight. "Oh, Jillian," she said, "like that, Jill, like that . . ."

We moved together, breathing as one, fighting gravity. I came first—lights and explosions and a humming sound in the distance that I realized was my own voice. I didn't want it to stop—the punch and pound of her knee against my center. As the throbbing dissipated, she, too, called out, saying my name over and over, and she could no longer hold us both up.

We slid down the door, me still straddling her thigh, my face pressed into her neck. My knees touched the floor, and she twisted, slid a boxing glove out of the way. She gripped me tightly, her hands caressing my back, under my arms, alongside my breasts. I felt the fire all over again. "You're good." I gulped. "Very good."

In a voice filled with wonder, she asked, "How did you do that to me?"

"What?"

"That! This." Her eyes met mine, and she looked completely flabbergasted. "How?"

"I guess you stopped fighting."

Mister Johnson gave Paige a job at the Shell station the next week. She worked there six long years until he sold it to her when he retired. Ten more years have gone by, and Paige still owns it.

And me.

SHIMMER

This story is dedicated with joy and appreciation to Victor J. Banis
who blessed us all with his writing, his wit, and his wisdom

Laurel's terror began, not outside in the unpredictable darkness among the crack dealers, con men, and thieves willing to gut a person for purse or wallet, but inside, at home, behind the locked door of her rowhouse in the supposedly safe vestibule where she and the other eleven tenants picked up their mail. The Ficus plant in the corner drooped, its green leaves withering from under-watering. A layer of dust coated the dull metal surface above the locked mailboxes. The hot water heat register inside the entryway clanked and hissed, and Laurel smelled the same familiar odors: old garlic, boiled cabbage from the Kraychik's dinner, and an underlying whiff of musty decay.

She removed a tire store flyer and the phone bill from her mailbox and smacked the metal door shut. Her fingers fumbled for the mail key, and that's when she heard him.

He came out from under the stairs, a ragged man, his jeans and sweatshirt soiled, black hair lank and greasy. He moved so fast she didn't have time to grasp the key before he was upon her. She opened her mouth to scream, but his hand closed over it. He grabbed the front of her jacket and dragged her toward the open area under the stairs.

Oh, my God, she thought. A rapist. Oh, God.

With surprising strength in his thin frame, he slung her in a half arc into the dark alcove under the stairwell. She hit the floor on her butt, sliding on the cold linoleum until her head and upper back struck the wall. In a low, raspy voice, he said, "Where's your purse?" His eyes were wild, his face puffy. He had to be stoned.

She shook her head. "Wait, stop—"

He stepped between the V of her legs and grabbed at the front of her coat. Laurel shrieked as she tried to fend him off, but he somehow got hold of her collar and dragged her sideways, ripping the leather coat. She kicked and connected with his knee.

He let out a roar. "Where? Where's the money?"

"Wha—what?"

His lumpy fist, stained with oil, hurtled toward her face. Pain exploded in her temple, her eye, her brow, her nose. How could one blow hurt her whole face like that?

All the fight went out of her. With a choking sob, she flopped on her side, moaning. Rough hands pulled at her, flipped her over until she faced the floor. Through one eye she saw the dirty tan and black floor, and then it seemed to telescope farther away. He lifted her by the arms, wrenching them together behind her as though he were trying to rip them from the sockets.

Laurel screamed. Her leather jacket peeled away, and she fell again to the linoleum floor. The impact knocked the wind out of her. She lay in a crumpled heap, her head pounding so badly she felt nauseated. Blood swirled in her mouth, and she gagged.

A draft of cool air washed over her. She lay on the floor smelling dust and feeling woozy. She must have blacked out because the next thing she knew, someone was speaking. She swam up out of confusion and fought through the horrible pain lodged behind her eyes. With a grunt, she rolled over and dragged herself to a sitting position. Old Mrs. Carson, in tan Sorel boots, thick Supp-hose, and a plaid coat stood in the passageway clutching the handle of her wire grocery cart. A gray scarf tamed her silver afro.

"Girl? Girl! Whatchu doing down there? You hear me? Girl?"

"I . . ." Laurel couldn't seem to make her mind and lips work in concert. "I . . ."

"Girl, I cain't hear you. Speak up." Mrs. Carson narrowed her eyes. "I axed you what you doing there? You hurt?"

Laurel swallowed and choked out one word. "Yeah."

"I be getting you the super."

The wheels on the grocery cart squeaked with such a high pitch that it sent a shiver down Laurel's back and hurt her ears.

My coat. He took my coat. Her wallet was in the inside pocket. She'd just cashed her check, and all her grocery money for the month was now gone. She sat for a moment, leaning on one arm and looking at the odd linoleum. The blue circle looked like a ring of gas-range fire, and the greenish oval was an olive without the pimento. *What the hell am I thinking these weird thoughts for? I've been robbed, and I'm focused on the floor?*

She scooted toward the hallway and rose slowly, ducking. At five-eight, she was too tall to stand up under the stairwell. On shaky legs, she took two steps, then grabbed hold of the wainscoting that ran along the hallway wall. *How had he gotten in?* Thinking of his strength and cold eyes made her shudder. Her head pounded even worse, and she shook partly from the chill and partly from fear. *He could have killed me, raped me. Oh, my God.*

"What's going on here?" The super, Mister Tidwell, had a nasally whine of a voice that entered her head like an overloaded bandsaw. He stepped around the corner, his keys jingling from a belt barely keeping his pants riding below his prodigious gut. "Mrs. Carson says somebody—oh! What the hell happened to you? Holy shit!"

The wall wobbled and wouldn't hold her up. Her last thought as she slid to the floor was, "I wish I'd been invisible . . ."

The first time Laurel awakened, the world was gray. A brisk wind blew into her nostrils and made her face feel frozen. She sat on bare ground, nestled between the gnarled, silvery roots of a giant tree. Outside the reach of the tree's branches, little pearls of snow whirled in a storm of gray flakes seeking a place to settle. The hard-packed earth was cold, and the frigid temperature soaked through her trousers to settle with an ache inside the bones of her hips and thighs. She crossed her arms over her sweater, hugging herself, and shivered.

She touched the trunk behind her; the tree felt warm. With effort, she heaved herself up, leaned back against the smooth bark, and wondered where she was. Overwhelmed by a bout of dizziness, she could barely keep from vomiting. Feeling miserable and sick, she gazed at the pewter-colored landscape with its flurries of snow. Where am I? What is this place?

She dared not leave the shelter of the tree, but she inched forward and looked out into the swirling storm. Abruptly her knees gave out, and she fell sideways into a ridge of snow that had drifted under the branches of the tree. As she crawled back to the safety of the tree's trunk, it occurred to her that though it was winter, the tree's limbs were covered with an abundance of leaves. Quicksilver in color, they rustled and shifted in the wind.

Leaves on a tree in winter?

She couldn't make any sense of it, so she took stock of her situation. Her slacks were wool and lined, and the ankle-high boots she wore would keep her feet warm, but she had no coat. And no money, no transportation home.

She heard a strange trilling sound, almost like a bird's call, but as it grew louder, she detected a lilting melody. That's no bird. Her heart beat fast with fear.

An outline in the blowing snow gradually became a man. His boots were covered with long, white fur. Tan pants were tucked into his boot-tops. His jacket was also tan, and he wore a white beret atop a head of light brown, bushy hair. One gloved hand held a thick wooden staff that he jammed firmly into the snowy ground before taking cautious steps forward.

For a moment Laurel held her breath, hoping he wouldn't notice her. But what if he was the only person for miles? "Sir?"

The man jerked to a stop and let out a shriek. "Who goes there?"

He did a full 360-degree turn, his face white with fear. He raised his staff and clutched it in both hands as if prepared to attack.

"I mean you no harm, sir. Help. I need help."

He leaned forward, squinting, his face twisted into a perplexed expression. "Oh! My, my, my. A girl." His voice was soft and high with a hint of an accent she thought sounded British. "How came you to this place?"

"I—I don't know."

"Poppycock. I suppose He sent you."

"He? Who's that?"

"The Bestower, of course. Who else?" He looked her over from head to toe and back up again. She felt as though he'd examined her inside and out as well. "He sent you ill-prepared. You're bloody small, too, if you should ask me." He smacked the end of the staff into the snow and grasped it with both hands. "Your name?"

"Laurel Miller."

"A miller in this bleak land? Wheat? Or Oats? Barley, I suppose."

"Uh, not any of those. It's just a name."

"Just a name? How quaint. How odd and quaint." He stepped closer, under the low-hanging branches and beneath the shelter of the tree's great arms. Now he was close enough for Laurel to see his blue, rheumy eyes, and she knew he was much older than he'd first appeared.

"Can you help me, sir?"

"You must, of course, seek the cloak."

"Is that anything like taking the veil?"

"What?"

She suppressed a smile. "I take it you didn't grow up Catholic."

"Bucolic, perhaps, but not the other thing you speak of."

"It's a religious term."

"I have no truck with religion. Too many problems." He stepped back and brushed flakes of snow from his eyelashes. "Seek the cloak, and you'll find your purpose there. Good day, then."

He turned, but she said, "Wait! I don't understand. What do I do?"

He made a clucking sound, "Listen, ducks, you mustn't seek revenge. But vengeance will indeed fuel you. There's nothing to do but seek the cloak and protect the unfortunate. That's all I can say." He trudged a few steps away, out into the blizzard of silver snow.

Seek the cloak? What the hell did *that* mean? "Don't go. How do I get out of here?"

"You'll figure it out."

"Mister! What's your name?"

She thought he called out that he was the groundskeeper, but he could have said Gary Keeper. Or Graham Sweeper. Then he disappeared into the storm, and there was no way to find out more.

She shook with a cold so deep and penetrating she thought hypothermia must be settling in. Her breath came out smoky white, and when she tried to rise, she gasped in pain. Her head felt like it was exploding from within. She closed her eyes and slipped into the silver tinsel world of frigid icicles.

The second time Laurel awakened, she lay flat on her back swathed in blankets. She still felt cold to the core, her head hurt, and something had apparently glued her eyelids shut. She struggled to open them only to have her vision assaulted by a bright light.

"Aha, you're back among the living. We thought we'd lost you for a bit there, but you're going to be all right." She squinted, then forced her eyes open wider. A man wearing a white doctor's coat slipped a silver penlight into his breast pocket and consulted a clipboard.

"Where am I?" Her throat was sore, and her tongue felt like a piece of dry leather.

"You've been in the hospital since last night, Miss Miller, but you'll be fine. You have quite the concussion, though."

The memory of the attack came flooding back. She sucked in some air, and that made her cough, so she tried to sit up.

"Please. If you could just rest, it would be better for you. I'll come back and check on you later. The nurse will attend to your cuts and bruises." He gave her arm a squeeze and was gone from the room before she had a chance to ask any more questions.

Hospital? She knew she didn't have the money for a hospital. She could afford her monthly rent, groceries, and heat bill, but there was little left over afterwards. Her job as a swing shift receiving clerk didn't offer insurance, and she had no nest egg.

Thinking of money made her head hurt again, so she closed her eyes and drifted off to sleep. The last image she saw was of snow, a swirling blizzard, and a protective silver tree gathering her into its embrace as though she were a small child.

After a week of convalescence, Laurel returned to work. She'd only been at the job for three months, so she was grateful her supervisor at the loading dock hadn't let her go. She'd been shy and had always avoided contact with the men, but now she realized the loaders at the import company liked her well enough. Over the next few days, several of them sought her out and expressed their concern. She was only twenty, and most of them weren't much older, so she thought it very sweet. Two of them even came in and offered to round up a posse and find the criminal responsible for robbing her. She had to tell them she was sorry, but his appearance was so ordinary he could have been half the guys who unloaded the trucks.

For a few weeks, an older worker who lived nearby walked her back to the apartment when they got off work at midnight, but then he and his family moved to another part of the city, and she was on her own again.

When she'd first come to New York during the summer from small town Nebraska, she'd been filled with a sense of freedom and exhilarated by the culture. Street vendors, yellow cabs, street corner preachers, delis and pizzerias with mouthwatering foods, and crowds of people bustling everywhere, day and night. She was glad she'd chosen New York. 1968 in the big city felt so modern, so hip. Though San Francisco's Summer of Love, the psychedelic music, and anti-war protesters had also interested her, she liked the Village and its restaurants and colorful mix of people.

But then in late autumn the weather turned cold, and she noticed the homeless, the panhandlers, the vacant-faced addicts strolling the streets like the living dead. The first time she saw a young man grab a purse and knock a woman down, Laurel had been shocked. Now, after her own attack, she was acutely aware of the desperation and feral looks on some people's faces.

On the way to work one day, she stopped at the Salvation Army store hoping to find a decent long coat. Since her leather coat had been stolen, she'd been wearing an old, too-tight ski jacket, but it didn't keep her legs and hips warm. After a few minutes of fruitless search, she went to the checkout counter and asked if they had anything not yet put on display.

The clerk shook his head. "Been a real run on the coats," he said. "Lot of sad little bums in here these last few days. I can always tell it's about to snow when they descend like locusts." He nattered on about the oncoming threat of snow, but she wasn't listening.

She sighed. She couldn't afford a new coat, for sure. As she turned to leave, the clerk said, "Hey, wait a sec. We do have some ponchos and absolutely amazing capes. The homeless never want them. Want to take a look at those?"

A poncho didn't sound promising, but she followed him to a rack next to the men's suits. He pulled at something made of silky brown cloth. "This is too light, but here . . ." He dug into the rack and dragged out three dusty items on hangers. He held out a fleecy poncho, tan and red with a herringbone pattern along the edges. She shook her head. It was small and wouldn't provide much warmth. The second was a black, bulky wool thing with a ratty velvet collar circling the top. Too heavy. But her eyes were drawn to a gun-metal gray cape slipping from his hands.

She caught hold of it as the hem touched the ground. An electrical shock zinged out and zapped both of them.

He laughed. "Feel that. Static electricity to beat the band."

Laurel took the cape into both hands. Made of smooth, closely-woven worsted wool, it had an upright collar and a hood as well. She'd never seen anything quite like it. Underneath the full skirt of the cape was another layer that could be buttoned up. Wearing it would swath her in a coat and jacket. She slipped an arm into one sleeve. The clerk tossed the other two wraps on top of the rack and helped her into it. The sleeves were two inches too long, but that meant they'd keep her hands warm. She buttoned the undercoat and arranged the cape around her. It hung past her knees. Perfect.

Seek the cloak.

Startled, she thought the clerk had spoken, but he stood there silently, examining the coat and brushing away bits of lint. She looked at him—really took in his appearance—for the first time. He was a slender, sandy-haired man with small feet, tight leather pants, a pink muscle T-shirt, and a cowlick in his widow's peak. One lock of hair hung down to an arched eyebrow. His eyes, when they met hers, were dark blue. "I think it looks fab. How about you?"

She touched the cloth at her forearm. Solid, but not heavy, it felt rather rich. The gray wool was dotted with silver and black, and as she stood there, the cape felt like it was generating warmth. She shifted and leaned and decided she could run in it without much extra effort. "How much?"

"You look like Family."

She stared at him blankly.

"Family . . . you know. A fellow sister to us nancy boys?"

Her face flamed. She'd traveled all these miles from Nebraska with the hope that no one in the big city would see into her heart, and a thrift store clerk uncovered her secret after a mere five minutes in her company.

He reached over and patted her. "No need to fret, dear. It's the shoes." Alarmed, she glanced down at her sensible oxfords. "Let it be our little secret, sweetie. I promise to keep it to myself." He named a price, and she pulled out her new wallet, which was still stiff and unwieldy. She paid him and left quickly.

The last thing she heard as she pulled the outer door closed was the clerk saying, "Come by anytime, Sweet Cheeks. Anytime."

Each night as she walked home from her work shift, Laurel enjoyed wearing the gray coat with the hood up and her hands in the slit pockets on the sides. Walking at midnight was frightening, but the coat made her feel hidden, almost invisible, even though she knew it wasn't so. She watched her surroundings with a sharper eye than she ever had before. Now she was aware that danger could come at her from any quarter, she was always on high alert. She thought often of the violent thief who'd attacked her, curious as to why he'd been that desperate, that cruel. She hoped she never ran into him again, but she saw him every day in the faces of men on the street, at the loading dock, in stores. She'd do a double-take, realize it wasn't him, and then spend several minutes trying to still her wild-pony heart.

Whenever that happened, her body felt less and less substantial, as though she were wasting away. And the periodic faintness wasn't only because she was short on grocery money and rationing her supplies to make it through the last few days of the month. She was indeed losing weight, but the ethereal feeling was something more. When Laurel was afraid on the street, she looked down at herself and her body seemed to shimmer in a gray-ghost way, as if she were disappearing.

After a while, people stopped noticing her. Nobody met her eyes anymore. Nobody stepped around her, saying "excuse me." It was as though she didn't exist.

She took to wandering the streets after her shift, often ranging far afield into both good neighborhoods and rough parts of town. She crept near the overhang of a huge bridge and saw homeless men and women warming themselves at fires burning in fifty-five-gallon drums. On one long avenue, at corner after corner, women in high heels and fishnet stockings stood shivering in coats far too lightweight to keep them warm. They smoked acrid-smelling cigarettes and called out to one another from across the streets, and when one of them was picked up by a man in a warm car, those left behind often cursed their own bad luck. She found a bar frequented by men like the Salvation Army clerk and looked in through one of the dusty windows, but she didn't go in.

Nobody noticed Laurel, and as time went on, she actually began to believe she'd become invisible. She often walked until dawn, then went home and slept past noon. She took care of her two-room furnished apartment, got her groceries, and read in the afternoons, then went to work. Her life began to feel small and cramped and routine.

A month passed, and the heart of winter descended. Snow fell often, streets were icy, and the temperature rarely rose above twenty degrees. Despite the weather, Laurel's passage through the city had continued uninterrupted, and her cloak kept her toasty warm.

But tonight the wind-chill was worse than usual, and she resolved to go directly home rather than walk around. Two blocks from her apartment house she saw a fat, squatty woman pushing a shopping cart most likely filled with her worldly belongings. Laurel had never seen this woman before. As she drew nearer, she realized the woman wasn't fat; she was padded with so many sweaters and coats that she just looked heavy.

Laurel looked up at soft flakes of snow wafting down past a streetlight. Out of the corner of her eye, she saw a motion and heard a cry.

The woman with the cart was down on one knee, whimpering, one hand gripping the cart's metal basket. Above her a giant dark shape loomed. "Gimme!" it said in a deep growl of a voice.

Laurel stopped, her mouth dry. For a brief moment, she wanted to run, but she found a spark of bravery, took a deep breath and hollered, "Hey, leave her alone."

The dark shape bent over the woman, and Laurel heard a shriek. The woman's hand came away from the cart, and the man rolled it forward on the icy sidewalk. The homeless woman slumped down and wailed.

The mugger pushed the cart ahead, half-jogging, and coming straight at Laurel. She stepped from his path, and as he passed, she stuck out her leg and tripped him. If he hadn't been holding on to the cart, he'd have fallen hard. Instead, his feet slipped, he was thrust forward, and his forehead hit the handle. He let out a roar, then got his legs back under him.

Laurel stood three steps away, sweating and panting, but he looked right through her. The man gave a shove to the cart and took off. Laurel glanced behind her. The over-padded woman blubbered and cried, but she was up, swaying on her feet. Laurel spun and followed the thief. He was now walking at a more sedate pace, nearly to the entrance of the corner drugstore. She caught up with him and kicked him in the back of the knee with the flat of her oxford.

He went down, howling, rolled over, and lumbered to his feet like an awkward bear. "Who did that?" he screamed.

"Who's there? Who's there?" He spun around three times, like a dog getting ready to lie down.

Laurel stood still, waiting for his eyes to light on her so he could attack. He stared past her. She peered up the street and back down. There wasn't another soul in sight. No one to help, but no one to hinder either.

The man coughed and sputtered. He grabbed for the cart. She kicked at the back of his other leg, but this time her foot glanced off, and he didn't lose his balance. His fist came swinging in an arc and caught her in the chest. For a moment she was airborne, then she crashed into the drugstore wall.

"I ain't been drinking," he whined. "What's going on? I swear I ain't had a glass for hours. Who's there?"

He advanced toward the wall, unable to locate Laurel, but all he had to do was get close and connect, and she was done for. Crablike, on all fours, she moved out of his path, wishing desperately that she had a weapon. She pushed off the ground and scrambled over to the cart.

"Who's there? Show yourself. Why can't I see you?" He placed a fist against the wall as though he planned to strike it, but he didn't.

"My cart, my cart." The woman came toward the man, her hands out. "Mister, please, give it back. Please . . ."

The thief's face was pale in the streetlight, but he wasn't spooked enough to run. "Piss off, y'old bag!" He shoved her, and she landed on her knees, whimpering, near the curb.

Laurel poked around in the cart until she came up with something long and black. An umbrella. She grabbed the top and hefted it. The wooden handle made a whistling sound as she swung it and hit his jaw. With a shout of pain, he stumbled aside. She hit him again.

"Ow! Stop!" He cowered, finally afraid. "Who is that? Jimmy, you playing a joke on me?"

Laurel lowered her voice to a rasp. "It's not Jimmy. Run, you bastard. Run before the Invisible Terror knocks you down and eats your soul."

She slammed the umbrella into the side of his head, and he let out a yelp. He tried to run, but his feet slipped out from under him.

"Invisible Terror," she said with all the menace in her voice that she could muster.

He panted and crawled forward. Twice, in his haste, he fell. When he finally managed to get up and stumble along the sidewalk, he didn't look back.

"You a spook?" The woman rose and squinted at her.

"No," Laurel said, gasping from exertion.

"You must be. You all silver and shit. I can make you out. Just barely. How come he couldn't see you?" She snatched the umbrella out of Laurel's hand and returned it to her cart. "I ain't had more than a bump or two, but I do believe I'll get the hell outta here. Get myself another whiskey. There be ghosts on this street."

She pushed the cart around the corner, and only then did she call out, "Thanks for saving my stuff."

Laurel held out her hands. The woman was right. They were a ghostly silver, barely discernable. She wiggled her fingers, but they weren't there. She stood on the corner, in front of the pharmacy, trying to catch her breath. The snow was falling harder, she was cold with sweat, and she couldn't see her shoes or her legs or even the coat and cape.

Her ribs burned, and it hurt to take a deep breath. Home, I need to go home.

As she trudged forward, the hood around her face and the front of her coat took on a faint, shimmery silver color. By the time she entered the apartment vestibule, she felt solid again. Her hands were visible, and the coat no longer shone that otherworldly color.

She went up to her apartment and threw up.

For the next week Laurel took the most direct route home after her midnight shift, but gradually her fear dissipated. Nobody gave any indication that they noticed her on the street, and as the days went by, she grew restless. By the time shopkeepers and apartment dwellers put up Christmas garlands and window lights, she was out exploring the streets again.

On a cold Monday, two nights before Christmas, she meandered through the West Village watching all the night crawlers. Men came and went from the bars, an occasional woman on some man's arm. Taxis arrived and ejected people clearly ready to party.

Laurel walked past a black door festooned with a white diamond. When it whapped open, letting out the thump-thump of a Jim Morrison song, a woman over six feet tall and dressed in a garish pink mini-skirt, fishnet stockings, and stiletto heels sashayed out and nearly ran into her. Laurel jumped back, narrowly avoiding a swinging, shiny white purse on a long strap. Laurel didn't understand how anyone could stay warm enough in so little clothing. The woman was heavily made up, her black hair a ring of Medusa-like curls. She glanced toward Laurel, who suddenly realized the woman was actually a man.

In the distance she saw flashing lights. Two police cars squealed to a halt in front of the bar, and a pair of officers with billy clubs emerged from each cruiser. Laurel stood rooted, not sure whether to run or make pleasantries, but the cops didn't acknowledge her presence. They passed through the brick doorway and disappeared inside. Abruptly the music cut out, and Laurel heard shouting. The black door slammed open against the brick, and men streamed out like panicked lemmings. She backed up against the cold wall, near a window, as men shoved past. A police officer followed them, swinging his billy club, and then he blocked the door.

Laurel didn't wait to see any more. She turned and ran and didn't slow down until she caught up with two men talking to the person in the pink mini-skirt.

"Damn cops," one man said. He and his friend both wore motorcycle leathers. "I'd just laid a twenty on the bar when they blew in. Probably never get it back either. Fuckers."

The other man reached out and gently touched the woman's arm. "Nina, honey, you got outta there in the nick of time."

Nine beamed. "That's my style—impeccable sense of timing. And look at the bright side. The Stonewall's probably safe from raids for a week or two. Bet they don't hit us again until well into the new year."

"That's not saying much," one of the bikers grumbled.

"No, honey," Nina said, "it's not, but I'm careful about things like that."

"You want an escort—make sure you get home safe?"

Nina smiled. From fifteen feet away Laurel saw the come-hither look she gave the men. "Only if you want to come up and have a little fun."

The two guys looked at one another. One shrugged and said, "Not really our bag, Nina. But thanks for asking."

"Ta-ta, then." She waggled blood-red manicured fingernails and strolled off.

Laurel followed her for two blocks and watched her unlock the door to her flat. Relieved that Nina was safe, Laurel walked on, thinking about all she'd seen. She didn't understand why a man would dress as a woman, but then again, she didn't understand why she longed to be in the arms of a woman. Since she'd turned thirteen, she'd thought there was something wrong with her. Leaving her hometown for the big city was the only answer she had come up with. She could hide in New York, blend in, be nearly invisible, which was something she could never do in Rushville, Nebraska.

She wondered how long it would be before the bar would open again. Would the police close it down forever? Or did it stay open after the raid? She checked her watch. Only half past one, so she turned and headed back toward the Stonewall determined at least to peek in.

Flashing lights passed, and a police car whizzed by, heading away from the bar, but when she got to the Stonewall, one cruiser still sat in front, its flashers alternating red and yellow. Two police officers brought out a man with no coat and hustled him up the street. The collar of his white shirt flapped in the cold wind.

Laurel paused at the bar's open door and looked in. The place was empty except for a man behind the bar who was sweeping something that sounded like broken glass. He looked up, his face tired, and said, "Sorry. Closed for the rest of the night."

"Oh."

"If the cops leave soon, I may reopen, but if not . . ." He put a hand to his face and shook his head.

Laurel's courage ran out then, and she hastened away. What was she thinking? She couldn't go in a bar like that. She shuddered, wondering what had gotten into her.

A great fatigue came over her, and she felt more than the usual emptiness. She had no friends. Her family had rejected her. Her job meant nothing. What kind of life was she living, walking the streets like a specter, always on the outside of other people's experiences?

She crossed a street and made her way past a four-story apartment building. An alley ran between the building and the larger one next to it. As she came to the alley, she was startled to see a police officer a few feet back, leaning against the wall and smoking a cigarette. She stopped. He took a drag as someone deeper in the alley let out a muffled shout.

Laurel took another step, expecting the cop to nod or wave, but he tossed the cigarette butt into a snowbank and crossed his arms.

"No!" a man's voice shouted. "Stop. God, no!

Laurel heard a thud, then scraping noises and grunting. Why didn't the smoking cop do something? Instead, he stood in the mouth of the alley looking out into the street and humming a tune. She took a cautious step forward, then another. The cop paid her no attention.

Soundlessly, she inched forward until she was near a chain-link fence that bisected the alley. Off to the side sat a dumpster heaped with junk. She kept moving. Beside it and near the fence were mashed up cardboard boxes and some kind of round wooden thing. She inched closer and saw a flurry of movement. Someone leaned over what looked like a huge wooden spool and struggled with a wriggling form below him.

She was ten feet away before the whole picture coalesced and she understood what was happening. A man, bent over and facedown, was pinned against the spool. His pants were around his ankles, and a police officer grappled with him from behind. Laurel moved closer until her toe came in contact with something. A gun-belt lay on a clear patch of cement.

"Goddamn you," the cop said. "Stay still!" He balled up a fist and struck the man in the middle of the back, then leaned in, jockeying for position.

"Get off me! Get away!"

The cop pressed forward. He wrapped a hand over the man's mouth, so the next shriek was muffled. With his other hand he fumbled with his pants.

Laurel couldn't breathe, couldn't move. A cop was raping someone. And the other cop was his lookout. She'd never heard of such a thing, couldn't believe it was happening. She held up her hands, feeling as though blood were dripping from them. They glowed a faint silver, then blinked out completely.

She squatted and pulled a billy club from the gun-belt. Gulping, she stepped forward. He seemed so enormous, like a giant blue bear smothering a small animal of the forest, and she wasn't sure how to hit him. The man on the bottom let out a scream of anguish, and without another thought, she raised the club and brought it down on the officer's head.

"Aaaaghhh." The cop staggered back and bent over with his hands on his knees. She stepped to the side and swung the club like a baseball bat. It whisked through the air and caught him on the side of the head. He let out a gargling sound.

The other man slid to his knees, his forehead pressing against the edge of the spool. She could see now his hair was blond. Laurel plunged forward and grabbed at his shoulder.

"No! No, don't," he cried out, his voice raspy.

"Shhhhh . . ." She whispered, "I'm here to help you. Get up."

The blond man let out a groan. Blood ran down his brow and into his eyes, blinding him. She leaned in and squinted, realizing he was familiar. "You. I know you."

"Not as well as that fucker does."

He whimpered as he fastened his pants, and suddenly it clicked. She'd bought her coat from him at the Salvation Army store.

From the end of the alley, the other cop shuffled around. "Hey, you okay back there?"

Laurel and the man froze.

"Smitty?" the cop called out.

"We've got to get out of here, past the guard." Laurel glanced behind them. The chain-link fence was at least twelve feet high and blocked off passage.

The cop on the ground let out a groan.

She grabbed the blond man's arm and tugged. "Get up. We have to run."

In a strangled voice, he said, "I can't. My ankle's turned. Will you get his gun? I'll shoot him. I'd be damn happy to shoot 'em both."

"No, we can't do that. Come on." She tossed aside the billy club, hooked her arm under his, and dragged him to his feet. She unbuttoned her coat and slung it around him, pulling him close.

"I'd have better luck with the gun, sweetheart."

"Shut up and stay with me." She hefted him up against her and took a step.

He let out a groan. "Oh, my God, that hurts."

"You can do this." She took another step away from the spool and toward the opposite apartment wall.

"Smitty?" Now the other cop strode back toward them. "Smitty!"

Laurel stood as still as she could. She looked down at herself and at the man in her arms. They both glittered faintly. The officer went down on one knee. "Smitty? What the hell? You okay, man?"

Smitty pushed himself up to one elbow. "Somebody . . . hit . . . me."

Smitty groaned again, and the other cop let out a growl of exasperation. "Dammit! I didn't get my turn. How the hell did you lose him? Oh, shit. Where's your gun?" He reached for the gun-belt. "Whoa. For a second, I thought we were screwed. Your gun's still here."

Laurel took a step toward the street. Then another. Her shoe scraped on the pavement.

The lookout jumped to his feet, his gun in hand. "Who's there?"

Laurel held her breath and clutched the man to her praying he wouldn't make a sound.

"Jesus," the cop said. "Must be rats all over the place." He leaned down over his partner and held out a hand. "Can you get up?"

Laurel didn't wait for any more of their conversation. She half-hoisted, half-dragged her charge to the street and hustled away from the cruiser parked down the block. She saw a delivery door for a deli, ducked into the alcove, and leaned the man against the closed door. He slid down to the cement. She felt like she was sweating every-where, but she was filled with a curious elation.

The guy looked dazed. He had a split lip and a cut on his fore-head, and his face was mottled with bruises. The streetlight illumin-ated the front of his white shirt enough to make it look like someone had splashed dark paint on it. She slid to a squat next to his legs. "Are you all right? How bad is it?"

He coughed several times, then gasped out, "How'd you do that?"

"Do what?"

"Walk us out of there."

"Just lucky, I guess. My name's Laurel. What's your name?"

He reached up with his sleeve and wiped blood from his face. "Roger."

"We might have to wait awhile, Roger, but after they leave, I'll get you a cab and take you to the hospital."

"Oh, God, no." He clutched at her arm. "I can't . . . what he did to me . . . No one can ever know. I can't even believe you know."

"You're hurt—"

He shook his head, his eyes pleading. "The hospital will report it to the cops. They'll find me. Find you. No hospital." He sagged back against the door and closed his eyes.

She watched for the police cruiser to drive off. Minutes ticked by, and she didn't know where the cops were. What if they came back, scouring the neighborhood for them? Soon Roger was shaking with the cold, and she worried he'd go into shock. When a yellow cab came by, she stepped out, hailed it, and managed to get him in.

Laurel cleaned up Roger's facial cuts and gave him ice for various bruises. He was settled on her shabby brown couch, his sprained ankle elevated on a pillow. She lowered herself into the only other chair in the room.

"Should we get you to the hospital for, uh, any other injuries I can't see?"

"No." He flushed red. "I'm okay. Sorry I wasn't more help. I was so woozy. Jeez, for a little while there, I was so out of it I thought you were some kind of invisible force. And this damn ankle didn't help matters either."

"I'm just glad you're safe." Laurel rose and went to her chest of drawers and pulled out an oversize red flannel shirt. "Why don't you get out of that bloody mess. You can borrow this." She tossed the shirt on the arm of the couch.

He pressed a damp washrag to his lip with one hand while unbuttoning his shirt with the other. "Those fuckers." His eyes filled with tears.

"Don't take this wrong, Roger, but why do you go to that bar?"

He twisted his fist around the washrag and gripped it so hard his knuckles went white. "Why shouldn't we have a place we can go to, some place where the pigs will leave us alone?"

"But it's dangerous."

"Dangerous? You should talk. What the hell are you doing wandering around the Village at two a.m.?"

She shrugged. "I don't know."

"I'm glad you were there, but you've got a lot more to fear at night than I do."

She paced as he changed shirts. "Roger, I can hardly believe cops would do that—commit that brutality. It's not human. They should be jailed."

"Tell me about it. And that kind of shit happens too damn often. I just never . . ." He paused, then finished softly. "I never thought it would happen to me."

They sat quietly for a few moments, and then his eyes sought her gaze. "Thank you, Sweet Cheeks. You give me hope that maybe there is a little bit of goodness in this fucked-up world."

They talked through the night, and when the sun came up a few hours later, Laurel knew she had a friend.

New Year, 1969, wasn't remarkable, except Roger gave her an old record player and the record album, "The Magic of Judy Garland." All through the rest of the winter and into spring, she roamed the streets at night in the gray cloak with the tune of "The Old Devil Moon" in her head. Every few nights she came upon a robbery, an altercation, an attack, and she interceded as best she could. She never found the police committing atrocities again, but plenty of others on the street did. The violence people did sickened her, but her ability to prevent crimes or punish the wrongdoer gave her some measure of peace.

She finally did scare one repeat offender right out of the neighborhood. Whenever she found the predator prowling the streets, she crept up behind him and whispered, "Invisible Terror. We're going to get you." She tossed things at him, tripped him, and tried to be as big a nuisance as possible. A couple weeks later she realized she hadn't seen him at all. He'd moved on.

Roger welcomed her into his circle of friends, mostly gay men, but also introduced her to a pair of older lesbians who urged her to allow them to set her up on blind dates with young women they knew. She promised to think about it.

She went to a party every week or so with Roger and enjoyed talking to people, but she was still shy. After Roger saw how reticent she was, he insisted on taking her to a drag show. "Open your eyes, Laurel," he said. "This is our community. You'll have a blast." And she did.

In June, he convinced her to go out dancing with him, but it took more than one beer to get her out on the floor so he could teach her some moves. They went to concerts and to gay music jams in Village nightclubs. But the one performer Roger wanted to see in person and never had was Judy Garland, and he spoke about her incessantly. At his apartment, if Laurel wanted to listen to any record, first she had to remove "Judy: Live at Carnegie Hall" from the turntable.

"Do you listen to anything else, Roger? How about a little Joan Baez or The Beatles?"

"Nobody compares with Judy," he said from the bedroom. "Oh, please. What happened to that Aretha Franklin album you had?"

"Lent it out. Just crank up Miss Garland." He sang the first words of "Come Rain or Come Shine," then said, "I'm almost dressed. I'll be out in a moment."

Laurel turned on the record player. Before she could set the needle on the record, someone banged on the door and Roger's friends Stan and Marcus pushed in. Both were agitated and out of breath.

"Where's Roger?" Stan asked.

"I'm right here, darlings." Roger came out of the bedroom dressed in blue and white striped pants and a strange-looking peasant-type blouse.

Stan broke down crying.

"What's the matter?" Roger asked.

Mark said, "It's about Judy. It's bad. Sit down."

"Just tell me."

"She died last night. She's dead."

"It's not possible," Roger said. He looked back and forth between Stan and Marcus.

"It's all over the radio. Overdose of barbiturates—something like that. Exactly like Marilyn."

Roger trembled and the ruffles on the arms of his blouse trembled with him. Then he burst into tears. The three men flopped down in various chairs around the living room. Laurel was amazed at how upset they were. They hadn't even known Judy Garland.

In the kitchen she got four glasses and a bottle of Scotch. From the living room she heard the first strains of "A Foggy Day."

She thought it was going to be a long night.

After five days of the tears, the tales, the histrionics of the homosexuals in crisis, Laurel found the neighborhood nearly deserted, likely because every gay man in New York City had gone to the funeral to pay their respects to the great Judy Garland. Laurel wandered silent streets in the afternoon sun and arrived at the loading docks fifteen minutes early.

After work, Roger was waiting for her outside. "Hey," she said, "was the funeral all right?"

"Sad, Laurel. The saddest thing I've ever seen. I cried so hard I don't think I'll be able to cry again for days. I couldn't get close enough to see her, but I left her a dozen red roses. You should have seen the flowers. Thousands, no, tens of thousands, I bet. More flowers than I've ever seen."

Hands in pockets, he continued to describe the service as they walked through a very busy Village. The queens were out, talking about Judy and crying on the corners. The streetwalkers plied their wares. Party boys kissed in the shadows, but the mood on the street was draped in a pervasive feeling of heaviness. Laurel didn't fully understand it, but the mood was contagious, and Roger fell silent.

As they approached Christopher Street he turned to her, misery etched in his handsome face. "I wish I could have heard her, just once." His voice broke. "I never got to experience her."

"I know." She slipped her arm through his and thought about how one person, someone you never even met, could have such a profound effect on people. "I'm glad you've got her records."

"Thank God for that."

They reached the Stonewall Inn, and he gave a toss of his head and said, "Come on. Let's have a drink."

She let him pull her inside the seedy bar. A haze of smoke obscured her view, and the place was packed, but the mood was subdued. She waited near the crush at the bar as he got two Vodka Sevens, then he led her to a table being vacated near the jukebox.

"Aren't you hot?" he asked after they got settled.

"A little, but I'm fine." She slipped out of the gray coat. The Jim Morrison song came to an end, and a new record clunked into place.

"Oh, God," Roger said in a strangled voice.

Laurel heard a collective gasp and started to ask what was wrong, then realized the jukebox was playing the first strains for Judy Garland's "Somewhere Over The Rainbow."

By one a.m. Laurel had run out of topics to discuss. Roger kept coming back to memories of Judy's movies. He wasn't quite crying in his beer, but close. A few minutes later, when "Somewhere Over The Rainbow" cued up again, someone called out, "No more. Please. We can't take it."

They sat for a while longer until Laurel finally said, "Maybe we'd better call it a night."

Roger rose, but before Laurel could get up, there was a scuffle at the front door. Someone blew a loud whistle. People all around her leapt up and rushed past, toward the back door. Others shouted in rage.

"Oh, shit," Roger said.

She grabbed her coat and had one arm in the sleeve when he grabbed hold of her and dragged her along the wall behind the milling crowd.

Plainclothes cops pushed their way in from the front door and the back as well. "Clear out," one of them yelled.

Laurel looked down to see one of her hands was shimmering. She tried to get her other arm in the coat, but too many people were pressed up against her.

The song on the jukebox ended, and the first notes of a new song played. Judy again.

"C'mon, Laurel," Roger cried out. He pulled her through the front door along with others who spilled out into the flashing lights of the police cars. Four cops stood waiting, clubs in hand. People were going every which way, and Laurel saw an open space. "This way, Roger."

Someone stumbled into her from behind, and a high-pitched voice shouted, "Hell, no, not this time!"

A beer bottle flew through the air, falling short of the police cruiser, and burst into brown shards. Another bottle, this time half full of whiskey, whizzed toward the front entrance. A cop ducked, and the missile hit the wall with a crash of breaking glass.

"You're all under arrest," one of the cops shouted. He brandished his baton and struck out with it.

"No!"

"Hell, no!"

Screams of pain. Someone pressed into her side. A man fell to his knees next to her. Her cloak slipped down her arm. A pair of hands grabbed her forearm as someone nearby begged for help.

A fist flew through the air, and she ducked just in time. She raised her hand to protect her head, then one arm was wrenched away, and her coat slid off.

"No!" she shouted. "Give me that—my coat. Give me my coat."

But in the mêlée, it was gone. She whipped her head from side to side, searching, desperate.

Nothing.

She shrugged off someone's grasp, shoved a leather-clad man aside, and pushed through. Where? Where did it go?

"Laurel! Oh, my God, Laurel." Roger hooked her arm to drag her away from the crowd. His nose was bloody. "I thought I'd lost you."

"My coat. Someone ripped away my coat." She tried to pull loose and go back.

He held her tightly. "No, hon, let's get out of here."

"I need my coat."

"I'll get you another one on Monday."

"No, I need *that* one." Tears came to her eyes. "I have to have that one. It's all that protects me from harm. I need it to help people. To help *our* people. To keep away the invisible terror."

Now they were half a block away from the riot, and Roger stopped to pull a handkerchief from his pocket. His face was alight with glee as he daubed at the blood on his face. "Not too damn likely. Look at 'em, Sweet Cheeks. They can protect *themselves*. We can protect ourselves. You don't need that coat anymore. We're free!" he shouted. "Judy may be over the rainbow, but we're in the here and now. We're alive and all right."

He grabbed her hand and pulled her down the street, away from the screaming and shouting and the ruckus. For a moment she could hardly breathe. She thought she might start sobbing.

Ahead of her, people were running. She heard sirens in the distance. "Stop, Roger." She led him up the stairs of a brownstone, and they stood pressed against the building, watching the brawl down the street.

"This is amazing," he said.

"No kidding." Laurel felt a stirring of courage. Roger's words ran through her head. *We're free. We're alive and all right.*

She didn't need to be afraid without the cloak. She didn't need to be invisible. From now on she would step up and speak out, live life on her own terms.

She gazed up at the row of streetlights stretching as far down Christopher Street as she could see.

The whole street shimmered.

About The Author

Lori L. Lake is the author of over a dozen novels and two short story collections. She's edited four anthologies, including *Lesbians on the Loose: Crime Writers on the Lam* with Jessie Chandler, which won a Golden Crown Literary "Goldie" Award. Her short work is featured in over a dozen anthologies including *The Silence of the Loons; Once Upon a Crime; Women of the Mean Streets*; and *Dark Side of the Loon: Where History Meets Mystery*.

Lori facilitates the Portland Lesbian Writers Group and is known for sharing writing craft resources. She is especially fond of teaching about crime fiction, short stories, and the craft of novel creation. In her spare time, she runs a small publishing house called Launch Point Press and administers the Alice B. Reader Appreciation Awards.

At the edge of Portland, Oregon, Lori lives in the Fortress of Solitude/Sanctuary of Solace where she spends time reading, writing, editing, playing guitar, adoring pop and oldies music, painting and coloring, photographing nature, and enjoying the exploits of her multitude of nieces and nephews.

Lori's Website: http://www.LoriLLake.com
(Lori loves to hear from readers and writers!)

Subscribe to Lori's Announcement/Newsletter
by Sending a Blank Email Here:
LoriLLakeWrites+subscribe@groups.io

Other Books By Lori L. Lake

The Gun Series
Gun Shy: Book 1
Under The Gun: Book 2
Have Gun We'll Travel: Book 3
Jump The Gun: Book 4

The Public Eye Series
Buyer's Remorse: Book 1
A Very Public Eye: Book 2

Romances
Eight Dates
Like Lovers Do
Different Dress
Ricochet In Time

Historical Fiction
Snow Moon Rising

Short Story Collections
Shimmer & Other Stories
Stepping Out: Short Stories

Anthologies Edited
Time's Rainbow: Writing Ourselves Back into American History

Lesbians on the Loose: Crime Writers on the Lam

The Milk of Human Kindness:
Lesbian Authors Write about Mothers & Daughters

Romance For Life

www.ingramcontent.com/pod-product-compliance
Lightning Source LLC
Chambersburg PA
CBHW060555100726
47907CB00005B/1364